Reese swiped the answer button and took a deep breath before speaking. "Hello?"

The labored breathing she hated brought tears to her eyes.

"I don't understand what you want. Why are you doing this to me?"

She yelped when her door swung open and Jackson's giant frame filled the doorway. "Hang up."

Since she was too shocked to immediately comply, he grabbed the phone from her hand and ended the call.

But his hand was gentle as he cradled the side of her neck and jaw and wiped away a tear with the pad of his thumb. "He made you cry."

He pulled her to her feet. Then he was bending, curling an arm behind her knees and the other at her back, lifting her off the floor.

Reese latched on to his shoulders. "What are you doing?"

"You're sleeping with me."

He seemed like a man who had made up his mind, and she wasn't a woman who wanted to protest.

SHARP EVIDENCE

USA TODAY Bestselling Author

JULIE MILLER

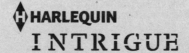

HARLEQUIN
INTRIGUE

To the state of Missouri, which was celebrating its bicentennial
(aka two hundredth birthday!) at the time this book was written
(not when it is being published).

Thank you for being the state where I was born. And thank you
for giving me so many wonderful places to visit and so many
interesting places to set my books!

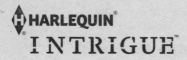

Recycling programs
for this product may
not exist in your area.

ISBN-13: 978-1-335-59137-1

Sharp Evidence

Copyright © 2023 by Julie Miller

Harlequin Enterprises ULC
22 Adelaide St. West, 41st Floor
Toronto, Ontario M5H 4E3, Canada
www.Harlequin.com

Printed in U.S.A.

Julie Miller is an award-winning *USA TODAY* bestselling author of breathtaking romantic suspense—with a National Readers' Choice Award and a Daphne du Maurier Award, among other prizes. She has also earned an *RT Book Reviews* Career Achievement Award. For a complete list of her books, monthly newsletter and more, go to juliemiller.org.

Books by Julie Miller

Harlequin Intrigue

Kansas City Crime Lab

K-9 Patrol
Decoding the Truth
The Evidence Next Door
Sharp Evidence

The Taylor Clan: Firehouse 13

Crime Scene Cover-Up
Dead Man District

The Precinct

Beauty and the Badge
Takedown
KCPD Protector
Crossfire Christmas
Military Grade Mistletoe
Kansas City Cop

Rescued by the Marine
Do-or-Die Bridesmaid
Personal Protection
Target on Her Back
K-9 Protector
A Stranger on Her Doorstep

Visit the Author Profile page at Harlequin.com.

CAST OF CHARACTERS

Jackson Dobbs—The crime lab's weapons expert. His life has been shaped by the unsolved murders of his parents, Dr. Everett and Melora Dobbs, twenty-three years earlier.

Reese Atkinson—Assistant theater director and PhD candidate at Williams University.

Maisey Sparks—The talented student is a thorn in Reese's side.

Zach Oliver—Prop master and student.

Patrick Brown—Set designer. He was a grad student back in the day, but he knew the Dobbses.

Dr. Dean Diamant—Director of the Theater Department and Reese's mentor. He was a professor twenty-three years ago and would have worked with Jackson's father. Did he eliminate the competition for a promotion?

Simon Lowry—Widowed benefactor of the department. He would have been there at the time Jackson's parents were killed. He's also Maisey Sparks's grandfather.

Dixon Lowry—Simon's son and Maisey's uncle. He's taking over the business and charitable activities from his aging father.

Chapter One

Jackson Dobbs left the Monday morning staff meeting at the Kansas City Police Department Crime Lab with his usual focus on the work he needed to accomplish. He rolled up the printouts with the notes he'd jotted from the meeting and stuffed them into the back pocket of his jeans before striding down the hallway toward his office, where he'd left his lab coat and safety goggles.

As a criminalist with the KCPD Crime Lab, he had a varied job. He was trained to report to crime scenes and collect evidence. Because of his inimitable patience and eye for detail, he was often called on to analyze reports and review tests conducted by other team members. But mostly, he was known as the Sharps Guy, the crime lab's resident expert on weaponry of all kinds, especially blades or other *sharp* weapons. He knew more about killing tools than the average criminalist, and he was sometimes requested to consult on investigations with other labs. He didn't have a kinky obsession with analyzing bloody wound tracks and gruesome crime scenes.

But he was far too familiar with all the ways one person could kill another. His life had been profoundly impacted by violence since and including the murder of his parents when he was twelve.

The *unsolved* murder, which had irrevocably changed his life.

Even as a twelve-year-old, he'd vowed that if he could survive his uncle's home, he'd find a way to help others the way he wished someone had helped him. Always the biggest kid in his class, he'd taken down bullies in school—then been punished at home for getting suspended. He'd been picked on himself because he preferred books over sports despite his imposing physique, and he could be freaky quiet, which had earned him nicknames like Creeper, Stalker and Mutant.

He'd been fortunate in high school to find a teacher who encouraged him to try out for football, even though his heart wasn't in the game—mostly because Uncle Curtis was such a big fan of football—and recovering a fumble or allowing the defense to sack the quarterback could determine whether or not he was "loved" at home that week. He'd enlisted in the Army to escape Curtis Graham's house, and to pay for his college degree.

After basic training, he'd been recruited for the military's Golden Gloves boxing program. The damaged facade that sports had started was completed in the boxing ring, giving him the look of an MMA fighter with a nose that had been broken and reset more than once, a scar through his left eyebrow, and two misshapen fingers from broken metacarpals and phalanges. When his stint in the military was up, he'd skipped a homecoming with the family that hadn't wanted him and gone to college to major in science and criminal justice. Then he'd gone to work at the crime lab.

Marriage and family had never been in the cards for him. Despite the loving example set by his parents in his early childhood, Jackson had too many strikes against him to develop a lasting relationship with a woman. Intimidating size. Ugly face. Working with crime and violence and death. Being an introvert. And an inability to process his emotions in a way most people understood.

But he had friends here at the lab. He had good memories from before and after his years at Uncle Curtis's house. And he was very, very good at his job.

He was assisting others by collecting and processing evidence that could help the police, local sheriff's department and district attorney solve cases, win trials and get criminals off the streets. One day, he'd solve the murders of Everett and Melora Dobbs. But for now, helping others was enough. His work at the crime lab gave him a reason to get up in the morning, and to use every skill he possessed to find the answers needed to solve a case. Because every crime he solved got one more bad guy off the streets and freed up the caseload of one more detective who might just reopen the investigation into his parents' deaths.

Jackson breathed out a heavy sigh that buzzed his

lips. Helping others. Right. People were counting on him. Maybe just professionally—but they needed him to do his job. It was the only reason anyone had ever needed him—to get a job done. And he wasn't going to let *anyone* down.

The first thing on his to-do list today was to process a handgun that had been found in a dumpster behind the Yankee Hill Road homeless shelter. At the scene, he'd been able to determine the gun had been recently fired. But with no reported gunshot victim or shots fired in the area, it was most likely a dump site. It was up to him to run ballistics to see if the gun could be matched to any other crime scene, and if it could be traced to a registered gun owner who might have reported it stolen or who might be a viable suspect for the KCPD to pursue. He'd ID the gun first— the serial number had been filed off, but he knew the chemicals that could restore the missing identification, if it wasn't too degraded. Jackson opened his office door. Then he'd test-fire a round…

"Hey! Excuse me?"

Jackson turned in the doorway. A petite woman was hurrying toward him, the ample curves of her hips and breasts shimmying a little as she walked. She had a big purse slung over one shoulder of the denim jacket she wore, and a paper sack with handles on it hooked over her other arm. Automatically, he glanced over his shoulder to see whose attention she was trying to get, but he saw no one in the hallway behind him. Everyone was either lingering in the conference room to continue conversations, or they had headed into the memorial lounge to refill coffee mugs and grab whatever snack they wanted to fuel their morning.

"Hello? Sir?" Her cheerful contralto voice called out again and he turned. "Yeah. You."

Jackson faced the pint-size dynamo again. Good grief. She was talking to *him*. She was making a bee-line straight toward him. Jackson felt the hackles at the back of his neck prick to attention and his muscles brace in anticipation.

Did he know this woman? Was she a cop or someone from the DA's office? She wasn't armed, and didn't wear that guarded air of wary alertness that the law enforcement personnel he knew did. She looked too young to be an attorney with her fitted jeans that were ripped at one knee, and her worn leather ankle boots. Maybe a law student? Had she been involved in a case with him? It couldn't have been directly. He would have remembered her short bouncy hair, the color of copper burnished with gold. Or the violet-blue eyes. Or the freckles dotting her face and hands like cookie sprinkles. Or curves that were almost too much for her short height.

He knew he hadn't dated her. His relationship history was next to nil except for a few friends with benefits encounters over the years.

Such was the love life of a man who was six foot four, built like a defensive lineman, with the distorted features of a prize fighter and who had a damn hard time speaking to most people. Especially a pretty woman. And this one was pretty. In a cute, shapely, all-American sense of the word. Like a breath of fresh air.

Or a hurricane.

"Hello? Did you hear me?" She slapped her hand over her mouth as a blush flooded her cheeks and blended the freckles away. With her face tilted to his, she leaned to the left and then to the right, studying either side of his square-jawed face. "I'm sorry. You're not hard of hearing or on your phone, are you?" She twirled her finger up by her own ear. "I didn't see you wearing anything on your ear."

She thought he was deaf? Preoccupied? He'd heard her just fine. "No."

"You're not on the phone? Whew." She smiled, and the light coming in through the front hallway's floor-to-ceiling windows suddenly seemed to pale in comparison. She thumbed over her shoulder toward the reception desk. "There was no one at the front desk when I came in. I heard voices down this way and thought I'd see if I could find someone to help me, and here you are."

She smiled again. As if meeting him was a good thing.

"She's pregnant."

"Who?" The violet-blue eyes blinked as she processed his terse response. "Oh. The receptionist at the front desk? She's taking a bathroom break? I hear that's pretty common when you're having a baby."

Isn't that what he'd said? That was the explanation he'd meant to give. But Freckles here seemed to understand.

"I didn't realize she'd be coming back. Should I have waited?" She held up the sack she carried. "I can't stay too long. I have a class to teach this morning, and parking's a bear on campus. But I didn't want to risk anything happening to this. It already felt creepy keeping it in my apartment last night."

Now Jackson was genuinely curious about whatever was in the sack. As a rule, his team collected, labeled and processed evidence themselves to ensure the chain of custody. "What?"

She handed the sack over to him, and he was surprised to feel the weight of it. He opened it to look inside and saw a rolled-up piece of flowered material stiff with dried blood. Clearly, there was something else in the bag with the blouse. But if this was something legit, he couldn't reach inside until he gloved up. Jackson's eyes narrowed as he moved his gaze to hers, asking for more information.

Freckles leaned closer to peek inside the sack. "I found it at the theater on Williams University campus. I was going through boxes with a bunch of donations. I thought it was a prop at first. But the more I looked at the blouse it's wrapped in, the more I thought the blood might be real. Stage blood gets goopy and gelatinous after it sits for a while. This is different. I assumed I should turn it in to someone who knows what to do with it. To look at it. Analyze it. Frankly, it's a little disturbing." She rolled her eyes. "Actually, it's a lot disturbing."

Jackson nodded. Generally, a concerned citizen called the police when they discovered something like this. He wondered what had prompted this woman to deliver it to the crime lab herself. "Looks like blood."

She pulled back to clasp the strap of her small duffel bag of a purse and shrugged. "I'm certainly no expert. You are. I hope."

Actually, his friend Grayson Malone was the blood expert here. He should direct her to Gray's office. But his brain short-circuited for a moment when she reached out and briefly brushed her fingers against the bare skin of his forearm before latching on to her purse again.

"Sorry. I should back up. I'm Reese Atkinson."

Reese? Now why did that name sound familiar? He was going back to the idea that she might have been a witness or a suspect or even a victim on a case he'd worked. But wouldn't he have remembered all those freckles and red hair?

"I'm an assistant professor at the Williams University Theater."

Jackson's speculation ceased and his jaw clenched at the mention of the place where his parents had once worked—and where they'd been killed. Did she know about his parents? Did she think her find was related to a twenty-three-year-old case? But if this woman picked up on his distress, she didn't let on. Or maybe his discomfort was the reason she kept right on talking. He knew he could put off a scary vibe when he got upset. Maybe she thought that if she spit everything out as quickly as possible, the conversation would end sooner and she could leave.

Maybe she was just as stressed out about making this report as he was hearing it.

"I'm directing a show there now, an Agatha Christie murder mystery. It's part of my doctoral work. At first, I thought this was someone's idea of another practical joke."

His radar pinged with the detail that slipped into her conversation. "*Another* joke?"

She shook her head, waving aside his query. "Long story. Someone has been playing games with me. I'm sure he or she thought it would be funny to hear me scream. Not that I did. It was more of a gasp and a couple of unladylike words. At any rate, if they truly wanted me to find it, why bury it in a pile of boxes behind the stage? Why not leave it in my office again?"

Again? What games was she referring to?

"Or onstage? Everyone knows I'm the first one to arrive and the last one to leave rehearsals." Shaking her head had loosened some of her hair so that it fell onto her face. She tucked her copper curls behind her ears. One of them sprang back onto the apple of her cheek and Jackson wanted to touch it.

He wanted to see if it was as soft as it looked, and if her skin was cool like porcelain or warm like the tiny spots that dotted her face. He carefully tightened his grip around the handles of the sack, willing the urge to leave his fingers.

"Dr. Diamant has been on my case about the backstage area being a mess—for Pete's sake, we're building sets and pulling costumes and running secondary rehearsals back there. Of course, it's going to be messy.

But he wants to have a party at the theater and have everything look nice. So, yesterday I stayed late to carry the boxes of recent donations from one of our patrons upstairs to get those out of the way, at least, since they aren't related to my show. I started sorting through the boxes—I pitched a couple of 1970s prom dresses that would only fit someone who was a size zero, and I hung up some other things we might be able to use." She paused for a breath and shied away from the sack he now held, hugging her arms beneath her breasts. "Then I found those. The material was wrapped around it, so I brought both."

"Around what?"

"The knife."

Knife? Williams University Theater? Blood? A chill ran down from his head to the toes of his work boots. In the very next breath, the heat of grief, anger and frustration that he'd buried inside for twenty-three years poured through him. The memories of all he had lost, and couldn't yet understand, buffeted him on all sides.

Reese Atkinson pulled her bottom lip between her teeth in an unspoken apology before holding up the finger and thumb of her right hand. "FYI, if you find my fingerprints on it, it'll be just these two fingers on the tip of the handle. That's how I picked it up. That's when I realized it was too heavy to be a prop. The blade didn't retract, and I thought the blood looked real, so I rolled it back up in the blouse where I found it, and decided to show someone who dealt with, you know, evidence things."

"Evidence things?" He pushed aside his emotions to stay with the conversation.

She nodded. "Crime lab stuff. I know television isn't always accurate, but I've seen shows where they put things in a paper sack and try not to touch anything so you don't transfer your own DNA or trace from your body onto what may be a significant clue to help solve a crime." She gestured to Jackson. "Then it goes to you guys at the crime lab."

"Pretty accurate." Television gave an unrealistic view of the speed with which tests were run, and how quickly conclusive results could be verified. But she had the basic facts right. "A certified criminalist should collect the evidence."

"I don't know any. Well, except you now. You're a certified criminalist, right?"

Jackson nodded.

"You're thinking I should have called the police?" Her red-gold eyebrows arched with an apology, and she gnawed on that full bottom lip again.

Reese Atkinson had such an expressive face. He could read every emotion there, from her worries about the knife and bloody blouse being some kind of sick joke to the nervousness she was feeling right now. He even saw her shoulders lift and her facial muscles still as she calmed herself and took on a more detached, professional demeanor.

"I considered it for about two seconds. But it wasn't like there was a crime scene at the theater. And I really don't need any more trouble with my show or want to explain to Dr. Diamant why the police were at the theater so late last night."

Jackson shifted with a concern he didn't want to feel because it wasn't his place to do anything about it. But was Reese saying that she had been in the theater by herself in the middle of the night? Where was campus security? Where were the people who cared about her? "You were there late?"

"Last one to leave, remember?" She raked her fingers through her hair, as if she was shaking off a bad memory. "I didn't think I should leave that lying around where someone might hurt themselves, or it could disappear."

"It's safer here." The situation wasn't ideal, as she might have inadvertently disturbed a secondary crime scene. Or, if she had nefarious intentions like covering up a crime that she or someone she knew had committed, then bringing the evidence to the crime lab herself might compromise any further investigation. "The police will want to talk to you."

She nodded. "I figured. I'm trying to do the right thing here, but I'm not sure exactly what that is. Like I said, I didn't want to make too much of a fuss. I don't need any more attention on me." She held out her hand in a friendly gesture. "Thanks for listening. I really do need to get to class."

She was still holding out her hand, so he shifted the sack to his left hand and swallowed hers up with his right. Although he intentionally made his touch as gentle as possible, she squeezed his hand in a firm grip that zapped frissons of electricity beneath his skin. Before he fully understood that little jolt of awareness, she was pulling away and pointing to the sack.

"I left my name and phone number in the bag, in case you need to follow up on anything. Or your police friends want to contact me."

He followed her gaze to where he heard footsteps behind him in the hallway, and saw his friends and coworkers Grayson Malone and Officer Aiden Murphy with his K-9 partner, Blue, strolling beside him.

"Looks like you've got company. It was nice to meet you, Mr... Um...?"

He swung his gaze back down to her violet-blue eyes. "Jackson Dobbs."

"Dobbs? Do I know you?" Her face squinched up into an adorable little frown. "Usually, I'm good with faces."

Since he didn't have an answer for her, he didn't say anything.

"Oh, well. It'll come to me."

Her pretty smile aimed up at him distracted him for a moment. But he was never distracted enough to forget the job. He reached behind him to pull out his wallet and handed her a business card with the crime lab logo and his contact information. "Here."

She skimmed the pertinent information before tucking the card into the bottomless pit of her purse. "Jackson—cool name. Thank you for your help."

With one last dazzling smile, she turned and hurried toward the front door, leaving Jackson standing there. She paused to introduce herself to Heather, the front desk receptionist, before looking back at Jackson and wiggling her fingers in a wave good-bye. Then she pushed open the glass doors and disappeared into the crisp autumn sunshine.

Feeling an urgent flare of curiosity, Jackson carried the sack into his office and set it on his desk before retrieving a pair of sterile gloves from the lab coat hanging on his closet door. By the time he had pulled on the gloves, Gray, Aiden and Blue had walked in behind him.

Blue, a Belgian Malinois, who considered the crime lab offices his second home, hopped up onto the small couch in Jackson's office. The dog pulled the blanket off the back of the couch, pawed it into a nest and plopped down to take a nap. Jackson heard the distinctive sound of Grayson's prosthetic legs and crutches as he came up on one side of him. Aiden turned and propped his backside against the desk on the other side.

The uniformed officer was grinning from ear to ear as he mimicked the wave Reese had given him on her way out. "You been holding out on us, big guy? Who's the redhead?"

Jackson pulled open the bag and snapped a picture of the contents with his cell phone. "Reese Atkinson from Williams University."

"Who's that?" Grayson asked, equally curious about Jackson's unexpected visitor.

"No idea."

Aiden chuffed him on the shoulder. "Man, you suck at giving us the scoop on your love life."

What love life? Aiden had married Jackson's team supervisor the previous Christmas, and Grayson was now engaged to the woman who had lived next door to him, and been his physical therapist. Jackson liked and admired both women, but he wasn't holding his breath that he was going to find the same sort of happily-ever-after for himself.

Once it became clear that Jackson was more focused on the contents of the sack than on answering their teasing questions, Grayson asked, "Other than the fact that she was cute enough that even you had to notice, what did she want?"

"Dropped this off." Jackson flattened the sack after he pulled out the rolled-up ball of clothing, and he carefully set it down on the clean brown paper.

With a long, low whistle, Aiden straightened when he saw all the blood. "What's that?"

"She thinks it's evidence."

"Of what?" Aiden asked.

Jackson carefully unwound the stiff bloodstained blouse.

"You'll be sending that to me for analysis?" Gray asked.

Jackson nodded, studying the long steel item inside. Although it was caked with blood and tarnished with age, he could make out the basic details of a Bowie knife with an eight-to-nine-inch blade and a cross guard to protect the user's hands. "A collector's weapon," he surmised, knowing the design was too impractical to carry on a belt or in a boot. Military and hunting knives tended to be shorter, and might have a serrated edge. Plus, their handles were made of a polypropylene or other polymers rather than wood wrapped in leather like this one.

"An antique?" Grayson clarified. "Something old used for a more modern crime?"

A wave of something familiar prickled the nape of Jackson's neck. "Don't know."

Aiden voiced the concern Jackson probably should have. "That's not her blood, is it? Is she all right?"

"Said she found it." Jackson opened his closet to retrieve his crime scene kit. He pulled out a couple of evidence bags to stow and label the knife and blouse. "Saw no injury on her."

Just smiles and freckles. Soft curly hair and sweet womanly curves.

"She found it at the theater?" Gray's investigative mind seemed to be heading down the same path as Jackson's suspicions.

"Yeah."

Grayson swore. He knew the history of the Dobbses' unsolved murder. Over the years they'd worked together, he'd helped Jackson run a few off-the-books tests that had amounted to nothing. "That hasn't been in our chain of custody," Grayson pointed out. "You need to follow up on it. Get pictures of where it was found. Take statements from any witnesses."

"Just her. She found it."

"Hell, Jackson. Are you thinking...? Your parents?"

"That weapon was never found."

Aiden interrupted the back-and-forth volleys of

the criminalists' suspicions. "What are you two talking about?"

"His parents were murdered in the parking lot outside the Williams University Theater," Grayson explained.

"I thought that happened years ago."

"Twenty-three." Jackson felt a little light-headed as he sealed the bags. A clue like this hadn't dropped into his lap before. Why would it show up now? If it even was connected to his parents' murders. "Stabbed to death. A few suspects were questioned, but no one was ever arrested. KCPD never did get their hands on the knife." He passed the bags over to Grayson. "Can you process the blood that's on the blade? See if it's a match to Mom or Dad? I can give you a sample of my blood if you need it for comparison."

"Murder cases remain open until they're solved. They'll be in the system." Grayson squeezed Jackson's shoulder, reminding him not to get his hopes up. "But you know it's a long shot."

"Reese found it in a box of clothing from the '70s. Older than the murders, I know, but who knows how many years the knife has been sitting in that box? Where did it come from?" Jackson peeled off his gloves and chucked them into the trash. "Or if someone recently hid it in there, then they have access to the theater."

"Chelsea could compile a list of names," Grayson suggested, referring to the lab's resident computer guru. "Students, faculty, staff."

"Does she know where the box came from?" Aiden asked. Like a good cop, he'd pulled out his notebook and was already jotting down information to generate a report.

"Donation." Jackson grabbed his leather jacket off the back of his chair.

Grayson followed him to the door. "Where are you going?"

"Williams University Theater."

"You think this is a lead?"

If not, it was a damn cruel coincidence. He was either going to find a lead toward solving his parents' murders, or rule out the possibility of hope.

Jackson had a feeling that, either way, Reese Atkinson was the key to determining which answer he'd find.

Chapter Two

"You have to break it during every show? That sucks."

Reese tried not to feel cornered by the younger man. He'd stopped her at the stairs leading up to the apron of the stage after she'd dismissed her Theater in Society class. But she was leaning back, and would have to sit on the middle step to avoid making physical contact if he came any closer.

She put up her hand to ask him to take a step back. "A little room, please, Zach."

"That's not fair."

She knew Zach Oliver was barely out of his teens, and that her show was his first Williams University assignment as property master, so he was still learning the ropes about doing a production that was more professional than those he'd worked on in high school. Yet it annoyed her that instead of making an appointment to discuss this during her office hours, or before or after rehearsal that evening, he'd started this conversation now. His fellow students hadn't even cleared the auditorium, and she hadn't had a chance to gather her bag and lecture notes. If she thought he was the conniving, dangerous sort, like the creeper who'd been leaving her cryptic messages and unwanted gifts, she might have suspected he was trying to catch her off guard and intimidate her into acquiescing to his demands. She also tried not to feel threatened by the way she had to crane her neck to look at him, since practically every adult male on the planet towered over her five feet, three inches of height.

Zach finally huffed a curse and propped his fists at his waist before taking one small step back. This was worth it, right? She worked the extra hours and dealt with all the egos surrounding her in theater academia so she could end up with the title of *Doctor*, and people would take her more seriously. Well, not everyone. Mostly her coworkers. And her more problematic students. All for a little respect. All to prove she was more than just a cute face or a child star who'd never reached her full potential.

Reese breathed in deeply, schooling her patience and remembering that she was the adult here—the teacher, an assistant professor of theater arts, a soon-to-be PhD if she could survive this semester and defend her dissertation next semester. Zach was the student, part of her backstage crew on her play—if an understandably upset student.

His short dreads bounced against his dark skin as he gestured to the three-foot-tall gargoyle sculpted out of two-by-fours and papier-mâché sitting on the edge of the stage. "Do you know how many hours

I put into making that?" Zach whined. "I thought you'd like it."

"I'm sorry, Zach." There was no arguing that the young man had created a work of art that looked as if he'd pulled it off the surviving parapets at Notre-Dame Cathedral. "It's a beautiful piece. But the character is killed when a pediment from on top of the building is pushed off and it crushes him. We'll be dropping it from the fly space every show. That's why I asked you to make something that looked more like a piece of stone. Like this." She drew a quick sketch on her omnipresent notebook.

Zach snorted at her simplistic drawing. "You want me to build a cube?"

"Your gargoyle is stunning," she assured him, hoping to turn this misunderstanding into a teachable moment. "We can use it as a set-decoration piece. Or in the display window in the lobby where we advertise the show. But part of being the property master is that you find or create props that meet the needs of the show. What I need is something that looks like a carved piece of stone. One that doesn't have a delicate neck like your gargoyle that will break when we drop it."

"Why don't you just get a real rock or cinder block?"

"Think about it. I'm not going to endanger anyone in the cast or crew by dangling a real chunk of stone over their heads that could break loose, or be accidentally released and come crashing down and hurt someone."

Understanding sparked in his dark eyes. "It needs to be about function as much as design."

"Exactly." Reese smiled, relieved that he was finally getting the point.

Zach was nodding, and she could see the wheels of creativity turning again. "Back to the drawing board, I guess."

"Thank you. Study some of the architecture around the old campus if you want inspiration. And remember, I *will* find a place to use your gargoyle."

"Sure thing, Ms. A. I need to get to class." Now he was backing up the aisle, his temper cooled by her explanation. It was a small victory. But it was a victory. "Are you still up for knitting that scarf we need for the show?"

Reese reached into her bag and pulled out the knitting needles stuck inside a skein of marled gray wool. "Already working on it. I've got the matching wig done, too. Go. You'll be late."

Zach gave her a thumbs-up, grabbed his backpack and jogged up the aisle to the exit. As he pushed open the door to the lobby, the dean of the Fine Arts Department, her doctoral supervisor, Dr. Dean Diamant, entered the theater. He stopped to chat with a group of three female students who were laughing when he approached and drew him into the middle of their conversation.

"Dean Dean!" One of them greeted him before trading a light hug. Now they were laughing at his once charming but woefully overused joke about being called Dean Dean.

But when the dark-haired girl who'd hugged him glanced back at Reese, Reese couldn't help but wonder if Dr. Diamant was checking up on *her*. As dean of the School of Fine Arts, he had every right to sit in on any class in the theater, music, dance or art departments. But since he was the adviser for Reese's PhD program, as well as the senior professor on staff in the Theater Department, she was always conscious of his subtle evaluations of her performance—as a teacher, director of the current production at the theater and interim manager of the theater itself for this term.

Unfortunately, Reese needed to chat with the same young lady who'd glanced her way. Reese packed her knitting back into her bag and waited for the conversation to wane. When it looked like the three girls were about to head out the door, she called after them. "Maisey?" She waved the young woman down to join her at the front of the stage. "Do you have a few minutes?"

"Sure." Maisey flipped her long dark hair behind her shoulders, and waved goodbye to Dr. Diamant before coming down the aisle. Her friends followed right behind her, and sat down in the third row to wait for her. "What's up? Do you have some notes about Vera?"

Maisey mentioned the part she was playing in *And Then There Were None*, the Agatha Christie murder mystery Reese was staging. Maisey was a beautiful girl, and a talented actor, who hoped to make it big on Broadway or in Los Angeles one day. Just as Reese had once hoped to pursue that same dream.

Before fear and tragedy rewrote the journey of her life.

While Reese couldn't deny Maisey Sparks's onstage talent and enthusiasm for the theater, there were some real-life issues the twentysomething needed to deal with. "Did you get your paper done? I'm ready to hand the others back to the class, but I'm still waiting for yours."

The younger woman lifted one brow into a beautiful arch, and pressed her lips into a pout. "You gave me an extension to get it done and turned in."

Reese kept her voice low so that Maisey's friends couldn't eavesdrop on their private conversation. "Yes. But now it's a week past that extension."

"I'm focusing on learning my lines and creating my character for the show. I'm the star. The play ultimately rests on my shoulders."

No. A play was all about teamwork. Talent behind the scenes and onstage all had to do their part to make a show come to life. Even a one-woman show needed the expertise and support of a strong director and a dedicated tech crew. And this was no one-woman show.

Reese hated feeling like the bad guy here. She'd once had that same devotion to her theatrical career until the nightmare had started and she'd lost her parents in their fight to keep her safe. Afterward, she'd moved in with her newlywed older sister and brother-in-law and had been forced to rethink her priorities. She'd used her free time to work two jobs to help pay her way instead of participating in play after play. Still reeling from the tragedy of losing half her family on one wintry night, along with the sense of security she'd taken for granted growing up, Reese had given up her dream of treading the boards on Broadway in favor of sticking closer to home and what family she had left.

No longer a starry-eyed young teenager, Reese had gone back to school and rediscovered her love for theater in the world of academia. Now she had her hand in all elements of the theater, not just in on-stage performance. She enjoyed working with young adults, and hopefully was inspiring their love for the arts now and for the rest of their lives. She could support herself on her modest university salary, and she was happy. Mostly. She still missed her parents. She worked for a capricious boss. She had a sister and two darling nephews she adored. She loved her job, if not all the people. But she could get along with pretty much anyone if she had to. The rest of her reimagined life would fall into place one day, too. Love. A family of her own.

A bone-deep sense of security that she would never doubt.

One day.

Today, she needed Maisey to understand the reality of priorities in *her* life. "I appreciate your devotion to your craft, but you also are a student at WU. You told me you were struggling with your core classes— algebra and biology."

"I still don't see why I need to know those things if I'm going to be an actress." Maisey's shoulders lifted with a petulant sigh.

Reese repeated some of the advice she'd given when they spoke last week about the paper. "Anything you learn gives you a better understanding of the world around you. It helps you put yourself in the mindset of a character. What if you were cast as a mathematician or a scientist?"

"A boring part? I wouldn't take it."

She wasn't going to argue that there were many movies and plays that took something as mundane as calculating mathematical formulas or discovering a new element that had fabulously meaty parts for actresses. Maisey equated acting with glamour. "What about understanding numbers so you could manage your own paycheck and taxes, or make sense of any contract you might sign?"

"I'll have a lawyer and agent to take care of that."

Clenching her jaw at the young woman's sense of entitlement, Reese gave up on reasoning with Maisey, and laid out the truth that she *would* care about. "If you fail my class, and any other classes this semester, you'll be put on academic suspension. At that point you can't be in any plays here."

Maisey glared down her long, narrow nose at Reese. "Then don't fail me."

Reese opened her mouth to reply to the subtle threat, but was interrupted by one of Maisey's friends.

"You're not a real professor. Not yet, anyway. I've heard about tenure. You can be replaced, you know."

Maisey arched a trimmed dark eyebrow. "Maybe you should quit, and let someone who isn't jealous of my talent take over the show."

Jealous? Reese almost laughed out loud. Worried about her student's arrogant disregard for the dangers of the real world outside the theater? Yes. But never jealous.

Reese straightened to every bit of her five feet, three inches of height. "I'm not jealous. I'm a grown-up. I understand responsibility. I'm trying to teach you—"

"I know you quit the business when you were in high school," Maisey whispered in an unpleasant snarl. "You couldn't make it in New York and had to come back here and resort to being a teacher. You're jealous because you know I'm better than you ever were."

"You don't know my story, Maisey."

And she wasn't going to waste the cautionary tale on this young woman, either.

"Miss Atkinson?" Dr. Diamant strode down the aisle. The man was a striking silver fox with broad shoulders, salt-and-pepper hair and a neatly trimmed beard. She could admire the man's vast knowledge and expertise, but there was an air of self-importance he carried with him and hands that were a little too touchy-feely with some of the students that kept Reese from finding him attractive. He came up behind Maisey and squeezed the shoulders of the girl who was young enough to be his daughter, before asking her to wait with her friends while he spoke to Reese. "Is there a problem?"

Reese couldn't miss the smug smile that spread across Maisey's face as she plopped down in a seat beside her friends. Why did it feel like this conversation was now four against one? Instead of allowing herself to be bullied, Reese tilted her gaze up to Dr. Diamant's dark eyes and shook her head. "I'm taking care of classroom business."

"And upsetting one of our premiere students," he pointed out. "Do we need to make accommodations for Miss Sparks?" His tone said he was telling rather than asking. He glanced back at the three young women and winked before speaking to Reese again. "After all, her grandfather is Simon Lowry. He and his late wife are the theater's greatest benefactors."

"I'm aware." She was still sorting through the boxes of props and costumes that had been donated from Mrs. Lowry's estate. But more than physical items, she knew Dr. Diamant was talking about the endowment the theater was receiving from the woman's estate. "At the last staff meeting, we discussed renaming the theater after the Lowrys since they've been giving us generous donations for years. With her passing, we'll have the funds to remodel this whole facility."

He dropped his voice to a whisper. "Or build a whole new theater. If we want those donations to continue, I don't think failing Simon's granddaughter is a wise move."

"I'm not failing her. I'm reminding her to turn in a paper. I'm teaching her the importance of keeping her commitments. Every other student in this section has turned in his or her paper." She appealed to the bottom line her supervisor was so focused on. "Mr. Lowry is an extremely successful businessman. Don't you think he'd appreciate the university teaching his granddaughter that theater is more than acting or singing? It's a business. Directors and producers will appreciate her being professional and responsible."

His dark eyes studied her for so long, Reese clenched her hands into fists down at her sides to keep herself from squirming or looking away. Then he smiled, breaking the tension between them. "Of course. I'll talk to her. Maybe she needs help with her research. Or tutoring. She *is* more of a performer than a writer. You could allow her to give an oral report. I'll see what I can do to help." It sounded like support, but it didn't feel like it. "Make those accommodations."

Reese swallowed hard, pushing down the snark that wanted to creep into her voice. After all, she'd been an actress. She could play the role of a cool-headed professional, even with the subtle digs being aimed at her. "Are you making any accommodations for me? You put me in charge of managing the theater this semester on top of teaching two classes and directing this play, plus finishing up my dissertation. And it's *Professor* Atkinson, not *Miss*. I earned the title." Okay, so her emotions were getting the better of this performance. "And you can address me as *Doctor* Atkinson once I defend my dissertation next semester."

Dr. Diamant's handsome face lined with concern. "You assured me you could handle the pressure. Do I need to reassign your jobs to someone who doesn't lose her temper at the slightest provocation?"

"I *am* handling it," Reese insisted. "But it's not easy, especially if I don't have your support." She heard noises from the backstage area. Footsteps. Voices. A stack of boards being dumped into a pile. The testing whir of a drill or power saw. It must be time for Patrick Brown's stagecraft class to get to work on their set-building project. "And I didn't lose my temper. I was having a civil discussion—"

"Whoa. Who's that?" Joy Archer, one of Maisey's entourage of friends, punctuated her loud observation with the pop of her gum and pointed to the stage behind Reese. Maisey smirked while the blonde girl elbowed her. "We should be doing *Beauty and the Beast*. He wouldn't even need a costume."

"Then how would you turn him into a prince?"

"That totally would be a problem."

"Joy!" Reese chastised the catty comments before glancing up the steps to see Jackson Dobbs scowling down from the stage above her.

Okay, so he wasn't exactly a handsome prince, with a jaw that was a little too pronounced, a scar bisecting one eyebrow and a crooked nose that looked as if he'd been in one too many fights. Although that dour expression wasn't doing him any favors, he was hardly a monster, hardly deserving of that cruel teasing. And, despite the growing din of conversations and power tools backstage, thanks to theater acoustics, he had to have heard the girls' disparaging remarks.

"Hey," she greeted him. Once again, she was struck by the sense that he was somehow familiar to her, that they shared a connection she couldn't yet place. "What are you doing here?"

He answered with a grunt.

Jackson's gaze was locked on Dr. Diamant, not the snooty trio, not even Reese herself. The big man she'd met that morning set a squarish black briefcase with KCPD Crime Lab emblazoned in white beside him on the edge of the stage. That looked official. He shrugged off his worn leather jacket and draped it over the kit, all without taking his gaze off Dean. Why had he come through the backstage area instead of entering the building through the front lobby? Clearly, she wasn't the only one prone to paying surprise visits.

"Jackson?"

Before he could answer, the third girl of the group whispered none too softly, "Do you think he can sing?"

"Who cares? You see the guns on that guy? I bet he's big all over." Maisey said possibly the most provocative thing she could think of as she ushered her friends from their seats.

Reese couldn't help but let her gaze slide to the muscular, veined forearms revealed by the rolled-up sleeves of Jackson's gray canvas shirt. Her fingertips had been drawn to them that morning at the crime lab. Jackson's biceps and shoulders stretched the material above his elbows, just as his muscular thighs stretched the denim covering them. The man was built in so many fine ways. When her gaze drifted to the zipper of his jeans, her thoughts following Maisey's crude remarks, Reese grimaced and shifted to study the large booted feet that were at eye level. The man wasn't a piece of meat any more than she considered herself a freckle-faced cutie-pie. Although, she did find him…compelling. He was just so much more masculine than anyone she'd ever dated, or maybe had even met.

He made another grunting noise that could have been a sigh of embarrassment or a snort of derision, but the expressive sound drew her gaze up to his rugged face. She realized those cool gray eyes were studying her reaction and he was frowning. Reese pressed her lips together and gave her head a sharp shake, pushing away the errant hormones that, apparently, she hadn't indulged in in way too long. She was having such a visceral reaction to a man she barely knew.

Without an outlet, the sensual heat blossomed on her cheeks, and she remembered that she'd taken offense at the young women's objectifying conversation. "Ladies. Get to class," she ordered. "Or lunch. Wherever you're headed next."

The three young women oohed and laughed, their voices fading as they headed up the aisle in a flurry of giggles and whispers. "He's way too old…"

"I don't know…"

"Maybe if you turned out the lights…"

"Ladies!"

The fact that Reese felt attracted to the same magnetic pull of Jackson Dobbs that the girls were making fun of was a little discomfiting. She and Jackson might have met just that morning, but Reese felt curiously protective of him. Which made little sense, really, since the man had more than twelve inches and a hundred pounds on her, and could clearly take care of himself. But he'd been nice to her at the crime lab, even though she suspected halfway through their conversation that she'd skipped some kind of security protocol by approaching him directly. He'd listened to her nervous ramblings instead of sending her back to the waiting area. And since very few people besides him seemed to be truly listening to what she had to say today, yeah, she was feeling a bond with their taciturn, polite and unaccountably hot visitor.

"Sorry about that," she apologized. "They're barely more than teenagers. Don't always think before they speak. Are you here to see me…?"

"Everett…?"

Reese swiveled her gaze at hearing Dr. Diamant's odd, nearly voiceless question to find him studying Jackson with narrowed eyes. Dr. Egoist's skin had gone strangely pale beneath his tan.

"Who's Everett?" Reese asked. She touched his shoulder, concerned by the pain she saw etched in his expression. "Dr. Diamant? Are you all right?"

"My mistake." Responding to neither her question nor Jackson's unblinking glare, the older man shrugged off her touch, dismissing whatever thought had surfaced. Color returned to his cheeks, and he donned his more familiar I'm-the-boss demeanor—smiling and polite, but not overly friendly until he'd determined a person's status in his world. "The theater isn't open to the public except for show nights. Miss Atkinson and I were having a private conversation."

Jackson watched a young man jogging down the aisle and up the steps onto the far side of the stage, before he disappeared behind the scenery to join the noisy stagecraft class. Then he was looking down at Dr. Diamant again. "Not very private."

Reese was embarrassed, and feeling some of that temper her supervisor had mentioned, to realize that not only had her students overheard the dressing-down from her adviser, but Jackson had, as well. "This is Jackson Dobbs. He's with the Kansas City Crime Lab. Dr. Dean Diamant."

Another grunt. "Everett was my father," Jackson explained, finally speaking real words in a gravelly, low-pitched voice.

"Dobbs. Of course." Dr. Diamant's smile became more genuine. "The shape of the head reminds me of your dad. But the hair is shorter, the color of your mother's—and obviously you've lived a rougher life than Everett did. Except for the end, of course." Dr. Diamant winced at the words that came out of his mouth. "I'm sorry. We were all very upset around here when they were killed. Terrified for our own lives."

"Killed?" Reese's heart squeezed in her chest as a light bulb of recognition turned on in her brain. She'd done a show with his father ages ago. Soon after, although she'd been little more than a child at the time, she'd heard the rumors about the kind professor and his wife, who'd been brutally murdered in the parking lot beside the theater. They were stabbed and left to bleed out and die after a performance late one night. Over the years, some of the more fanciful students even claimed that the couple still haunted the place. And she'd brought Jackson back, to what must be a nightmare for him, by handing over that knife. Reese cupped her hands over her mouth, as if she could retract any hurtful words she'd said, or painful memories that she might have triggered in him. "I'm so sorry. I didn't put two and two together this morning that you were related—"

The dean interrupted her apology before extending his hand to introduce himself. "I'm dean of the School of Fine Arts now. I knew your parents. Your father and I taught together. He was a good man. A friend. Your mother worked in the fine arts office. Beautiful woman. Such a tragedy."

Slowly moving his gaze from Reese over to her boss, Jackson reached down over the edge of the stage to shake the dean's extended hand. "I remember you."

Judging by his scowl, it didn't look as if they were very good memories. Maybe Jackson hated everything about the theater and the university. Or maybe that stern stoicism was an unfortunate side effect of his scarred face.

"You were what—ten? twelve?—last time we met? Must have been at the funeral."

Jackson had no comment about Dr. D's tacky trip down memory lane.

"How about a little sensitivity," Reese protested.

But her boss was talking over her again. "You're with the crime lab now? Wait. Are the police here? Has something happened?" Dr. Diamant's gaze swept the auditorium before fully acknowledging Reese. With no flashing lights outside the lobby doors or uniformed officers inside to back up his concerns, he frowned, then reprimanded her. "I should have been informed immediately if there was an issue on campus."

Somehow the crime lab showing up in the theater was her fault? "No one is in any danger. Last night, I found something that I thought might be a piece of evidence. The fact that Mr. Dobbs is here now makes me think I was right."

"What evidence? To what crime? At the theater? Was there an assault? Have we been vandalized again?" He tilted his gaze to Jackson again. "We've had a series of break-ins across campus. Nothing taken. Just some damage. The Deans' Council suspects a fraternity initiation. Campus police have stepped up…" He paused and the color drained from his face again. "Oh, Lord. Does this have something to do with your parents' murders? I know the case was never solved. I'm the one who found them, you know. Your father was already gone. Your mother was badly injured, already unconscious. They were holding hands."

Oh, my God. How heartbreaking.

Jackson came down the stairs, one deliberate step at a time. "I know the details."

Reese had to back up when he stopped between her and the dean. She was torn between inhaling the clean leathery scent that came off Jackson's body, offering him a comforting hug and snickering at the realization that, even standing on the same level, Dr. Diamant still had to angle his head up to hold Jackson's gaze. She was ready for Jackson to ream out the older man for callously rambling on about his parents' tragic deaths.

"I need you to be a lot nicer when you speak to Professor Atkinson."

Professor? Reese was completely caught off guard by Jackson's pronouncement. Had he heard her mini tirade? He was defending *her*?

"What?" The dean's dark eyes darted from Jackson down to her, then back up again. Confusion lined his face. "Are you Reese's boyfriend?" Why would he ask that? Was that the only reason he thought anyone would stand up for her? After a moment, Dr. Diamant glanced at Reese. "Dobbs here isn't what I expected. You're a free spirit. But you're also an academic. He's a public servant."

"He's a scientist," Reese countered, hating the condescending note in the dean's tone. "Even if he was a garbage collector, my personal life wouldn't be any of your business."

Dr. Diamant patted the air, placating her, and lowered his tone as though her argument was unwarranted. "I just thought you'd go for a man with a more bohemian vibe—someone in the arts. I thought you were seeing Professor Brown?" It had been one date. One spark-free disappointment before they agreed they got along better as friends. But Reese never got the chance to correct him. "Of course, you and Dobbs both have a background in the theater, at least by association—"

"Now." Jackson sharpened his articulation without raising the volume of his voice.

"Now? Now what?" For a moment, the dean was puzzled by the single word. Then he offered them both a handsome smile. "My apologies if I offended you. Reese is a valued member of our faculty. And you're a bit of a legacy around here, I suppose, being Everett and Melora's son. It's natural for me to assume you two could be a thing."

Jackson grunted at the dean's rambling excuse for an apology before facing Reese. "I have questions."

She jumped when Jackson's fingers brushed against her upper arm. He immediately drew his hand back and tucked his fingers into the front pocket of his jeans. Reese felt guilty that he might have misinterpreted her startled response.

She was still processing the fact that this big bruiser, who had every right to lash out in pain, had stood up for her against the dean's disrespect. But she wasn't averse to a man of his kindness touching her. Watching Jackson literally put more space between them, Reese reached out and linked her fingers into the crook of his elbow, halting his retreat. Even as she stepped into his side and tightened her grip on his sleeve, she wondered if the vibrations she felt humming between them were tremors of surprise in Jackson's muscles, or her own barely checked emotions spiking through her.

"If you'll excuse us, Dean." Good grief. The man generated heat like a furnace, and Reese fought the urge to lean into him to soak up some of that warmth. "I need to speak to Jackson."

The dean nodded, pointing a finger at her as he retreated up the aisle. "Police business, then. That makes more sense. All right. As long as it doesn't interfere with class, I'll leave you to it. Remember, keep Maisey happy. I'll make sure you have something from her to grade."

She idly wondered if he'd recruit another student to write the paper for her, or even do it himself. Whatever it took to keep their theater angels happy, she supposed.

Dr. Diamant had exited into the lobby before Jackson dropped his gaze to the spot on his arm where her fingers clung to him. Then, leaving his face downcast, he tilted his gaze to hers. "He's rude."

"Sorry about that."

"He's rude to *you*."

Jackson wasn't a handsome man, and clearly, he wasn't a glib conversationalist. But nice? Polite? So male that women of all ages seemed to notice? And now he was showing how protective he could be?

Reese's hormones kicked into hyperdrive, even as that self-preserving instinct that was constantly on guard inside her tensed.

"Yeah. But he's in charge. Of my job and my dissertation." She shrugged. "I don't know whether to be grateful or put out that I've been arguing with him for months without much change. Yet you say one thing to him, and he suddenly listens? He's never apologized before. Of course, that's probably just because you're here. Because you're a *legacy*. He's always super cognizant of the theater's reputation and where our next donation might be coming from."

"Did I overstep?"

"No. I'm grateful for the support. I'm just not used to anyone fighting a battle for me."

His eyes narrowed. "You fight a lot of battles?"

"More than you know." Reese realized she'd been stroking the warm skin along his forearm with her thumb, tracing the path of one of the prominent veins she'd noticed earlier. Suddenly, she was too hot, with him standing so close and his gaze on her so intense. This man saw too much, more than he let on, and it was unsettling. She abruptly pulled away and circled around him to lift her bag off the stage.

"I wasn't offended by those girls."

She looped the strap over her shoulder. "Well, I was. Maisey comes from money, and she's spoiled. I'm supposed to be the one in charge. The professor. The director. The manager. Those are all titles that should command a little respect."

She glanced up to find him nodding. "If your boss spoke with more respect—"

"They'd emulate him?" She'd gotten his point, so there was no reply. "Thank you for standing up for me. I don't know if it will make a difference with Dean Diamant, but it made me feel better to have someone in my corner." She headed up the stairs. "Do you think that knife has something to do with your parents' deaths?"

"Possibly." He followed behind her, taking the stairs two at a time.

Despite the noise coming from the class backstage, they were now alone. Still, she didn't imagine being front and center onstage like this was a place where a quiet, socially awkward man like Jackson Dobbs felt comfortable. Especially if he was here to talk about murder. "So, ask me questions."

Chapter Three

"Someplace private?" Jackson suggested, stepping aside to let Reese stoop beside Zach Oliver's gargoyle.

"Sure. My office is backstage." She heaved the prop into her arms to move it to an out-of-the-way location where no one could, accidentally or intentionally, damage the work of art.

"That heavy?"

She led the way across the stage. "Not bad. The base is solid, but the rest is papier-mâché. Now that it's up on my hip, I…oh."

He pulled the gargoyle from her hands and carried both it and his kit without any trouble.

"Thank you. But I'm not a diva who refuses to haul my own set pieces. Could I at least carry your jacket?"

He ignored her insistence that she could move the heavy prop. "Where?"

"Back here." She hurried ahead to the trio of offices located off the cavernous workroom behind the stage, and unlocked the first door. She pointed to an empty spot on top of the file cabinet while she tossed her bag onto the chair behind the desk. Jackson had the oversize prop situated before she could get back to help him. "Thanks."

She saw her crowded office through his eyes as he swept the room for a place to set his kit before simply lowering it to the thin carpet beside his feet. Reese groaned. There wasn't even an empty chair where she could invite him to sit. Her desk held papers and scripts, research books, a framed picture of her sister's family and an old one of her parents, and a computer. The worktable was covered by a 3D model of her set, along with many props, including a judge's wig she had built out of gray yarn draped over a foam head, and a silver tray that held a broken decanter and several glasses. Another table along the wall was littered with posters and promo items from the previous season's shows and an old-fashioned portable record player, which was also a prop in the current production.

She felt embarrassment warming her cheeks. "Sorry about the mess. Chaos is kind of my thing when I'm directing a play. No time to organize."

"Creative." He nodded, as though that one word explained the mess and maybe even made it acceptable in his eyes. "Dad's was similar."

"Don't stereotype theater people," she defended herself with mock indignity. "It's not always a pigsty."

"Know where things are?"

"Of course."

Her answer seemed to be all he needed to earn an approving nod. "Dad, too."

She smiled with relief that he seemed to understand her messy system of organization. Reese moved to the guest chair on the near side of her desk, and scooped up the stack of costume sketches she'd laid there. "I bet your office is pristine, with everything put away in its own place."

She reached for his jacket to drape over the back of the chair, fighting the urge to pull its heavy weight up to her nose and breathe in deeply. She gestured for him to sit, and turned to find a corner of her desk where she could set the drawings. She shivered when she saw the manila envelope in which she'd stashed the messages that were someone's idea of a clever joke. They'd been left on the windshield of her car or stuffed under the door to her office over the past couple of weeks. Reese slapped the drawings down on top of the envelope. Out of sight, out of mind. They were just words, anyway. Words couldn't hurt her, right? Not on the written page, not in a mysterious phone call. They could undermine her authority or rattle her self-confidence—but they weren't physically dangerous. She just needed to endure long enough for whoever was getting their kicks out of this sneaky game to grow tired of messing with her.

Then she realized that Jackson was standing close enough that she could feel his abundant heat through her blouse and denim jacket. He towered over her, his gaze moving from her to her desk and back again, as if he'd sensed she was hiding something.

Right. She'd been apologizing for the mess and guessing his office wasn't anything like her own. She fixed a smile on her face before tilting her eyes way up to his. "Do you work mostly in your office or in a lab?"

"Lab."

"You don't talk in complete sentences very much, do you?" She could see he wasn't entirely at ease or given to making small talk, but since she wasn't feeling like her usual perky, extroverted self, she started the conversation she assumed he wanted to have with her. "The knife? Did it turn out to be something important?"

"I need to see where you found it."

All business. She could handle that. She suspected Jackson was more comfortable with an investigation-related conversation, although she missed the grumbly, low-pitched protective vibe of him telling Dean Diamant to be more respectful. *I need you to be a lot nicer when you speak to Professor Atkinson.*

Those words had felt like a supportive hand at her back, like Jackson Dobbs saw her as a grown woman. Being sheltered by the big lab geek's abundant heat—like she was important to him—made her feel as if he wanted the rest of the world to know that she wasn't alone in the battles she fought against misconceptions and intimidation tactics.

But this wasn't a date. Jackson wasn't her boyfriend. His visit to the theater had nothing to do with her troubles. And even though she felt an inexplicable connection to him, he was barely more than an acquaintance—although she couldn't deny being fascinated by him, being drawn to him, feeling more secure with him in her world.

Reese combed her fingers through the short curls that fell over her forehead, and shifted her thoughts back into concerned-citizen, theater-caretaker mode as she'd been that morning at the crime lab. "You need to see where I found the box it was in originally? Or where I opened and unpacked the box upstairs?"

"Both."

Reese smiled. He didn't need to say much when he could communicate so succinctly. She checked the chunky watch on her wrist, which had once been her father's. "I have a couple of hours between classes. You want to look now?"

He nodded and reached down to open his CSI kit. By the time she'd hidden her purse in the bottom drawer of her desk and retrieved her keys, he had pulled on a pair of sterile gloves and looped a high-tech camera around his neck. After locking her door, she led him through the noisy construction of the set pieces and flats being built by the stagecraft class. Since the man in charge of the class, Patrick Brown, was wearing noise-canceling earphones, she simply exchanged a wave of acknowledgment with the blond-haired professor and hurried through the sawdust, drills, platforms and plywood to the back wall where floor-to-ceiling shelves stored several boxes, large props and building supplies.

"Sorry about the noise," she apologized, raising her voice a bit. She put a hand on a large dented box on the bottom shelf. "Beatrice Lowry, one of the theater's biggest benefactors, passed away a few months back. About two weeks ago, her husband donated a ton of her stuff to the theater. She must have been collecting it for decades."

"Related to Simon Lowry?"

Of course, he recognized the name of one of Kansas City's wealthiest and most civic-minded families. "Yes. She was his wife. You know him?"

"Of him. My folks went to parties."

"The Lowrys still throw a holiday party for the theater faculty and staff, and host fundraisers for fine arts projects. I heard that their son, Dixon Lowry, will be taking over now that Beatrice has passed. He's Maisey's—one of the rude girls—uncle. They're holding an open house here this weekend for theater faculty and students to help launch the beginning of the main-stage season. I'm guessing that's when the dean will announce renaming the theater in Beatrice's memory." Reese retreated several steps and stretched out her arms. "These are the boxes I haven't gone through yet. They were stacked up out to here. They were a fire hazard since they narrowed the path to the back door, so I moved several of them upstairs to the loft where we store costumes and hand props."

He snapped a few pictures of the area, then pulled out the boxes and opened them. After taking more pictures of the contents and boxes themselves, he moved them back into place. Then he pointed to the commercial shipping label on the outside of each box. "The one with the knife was the same?"

She nodded. "Obviously, Mr. Lowry didn't haul these in himself. I assume they'd all been taped shut by that local shipping company and delivered here. I signed for them."

He traced the Williams University Theater address with his gloved finger. "It's been opened and taped shut more than once."

"So, the knife didn't necessarily come from Simon Lowry's home. Someone could have opened the box, put the knife in, then sealed it shut again?"

Jackson nodded. "Here, or at Lowry's end. No clue."

Reese frowned. "I'm sorry. I didn't really pay attention to that. I just assumed they'd been reopened to stuff in a couple more items before shipping them here. I broke down the boxes as I emptied them. Did I mess up your investigation?"

"I can dust for prints."

Reese paced for a bit, then shared a brief conversation with Patrick Brown about her choice of paint colors for the set. Finally, she returned to watch Jackson work.

Thorough would be an understatement. He spent almost an hour working in silence, poring over each seam of the boxes with a lighted magnifying tool. A few times he pulled out a jar of black powder and a fat, flared brush to dust a section of the tape or box. Reese knelt beside him to watch him press what looked like a piece of clear tape over the dust marks, and then carefully peel it away and adhere it to a small rectangle of white cardboard. He labeled it with the date, the object and location where he'd lifted the print, along with his initials, before holding it beneath his light to study it.

Reese studied the remarkably clear image, too. "Wow. Even I can see the ridges and swirls of a fingerprint."

"Thumbprint," he corrected.

Reese flipped her hands over and held them next to the card. "Not mine, is it?"

"Too big." He tucked the card into one of the many pockets in his CSI kit. "A man's."

"It could be from one of the movers," she supposed.

Jackson agreed. "Probably bonded, with prints on file. Chelsea will check."

"Who's Chelsea?" It was the first time she'd heard Jackson mention any woman besides the pregnant receptionist at the crime lab.

"Hacker." He packed the rest of his tools and samples into his kit, as well, except for the camera and a flashlight. When he saw Reese frowning up at him, clearly asking him for more of an explanation, he shrugged. "In charge of computers and research at the lab. Tech genius. She can find anything on the web."

"Cool. I wish I could do something useful like that."

Now he was the one frowning, and it hardened his expression enough that she leaned away from him. "You teach."

"I'm not exactly tracking down criminals or saving lives."

"*Shaping* lives." He cleared his throat before continuing in a harsh, gravelly tone. "Whether they know it or not, those students need you. The right teacher can make a difference in how a student's life turns out."

His emphatic response made her think he didn't appreciate her making light of his assertion. "Did a teacher impact your life like that?" When he didn't answer, she searched for a less dramatic explanation. "Your parents both worked in academia. I can understand how you'd value education."

"You…" He struggled to find a word, then surprised her with the one he chose. "…smile."

Reese arched a doubtful eyebrow. "That's useful?"

He quickly refocused on his work, as if he'd admitted something he didn't want her to know. "I don't smile."

"Sure you do," she insisted. "I've seen that little quirk at the corner of your mouth. It may not be a toothy grin, but I totally count that as a smile."

Not only was there no toothy grin, but she didn't even earn that lift at the corner of his firm lips. Instead, he snapped his kit shut. "How many boxes were there?"

Either she'd touched on a sensitive subject or he didn't like her flirting with him. And yeah, she was honest enough to admit that she'd been doing what she could to elicit more conversation, and a few of those smiles. Reese centered herself on a deep breath and tried not to let his swift changes, from polite to friendly to snapping beast to hinting at something deeply emotional and back to impersonally polite again, get to her. "Fourteen. I carried eight of them upstairs and opened them with a box cutter. Then I cleared the shelf space here, and stashed the rest until I could get to them."

"No one helped?"

"You're a little obsessed with me doing things on my own. I assure you, I'm a very capable woman." She braced her hand on his shoulder and pushed herself upright. Good grief. Why did she keep touching the man? His shoulder was broad and muscled and as seemingly unmovable as the rest of him. Reese quickly snatched her hand away. "Sorry. I should have asked before touching you. I keep forgetting my manners. I know I wouldn't like it if someone I'd just met kept putting their hands on me."

"I don't mind," he assured her. He stood. "I know it doesn't mean anything."

Was that why he didn't appreciate her flirting? He didn't believe she was sincere in wanting to get to know him better? Huffing out a sigh of irritation, Reese propped her hands at her hips. "Of course, it means something. If I didn't trust you on some level, I wouldn't be touching you at all." She pointed back to the stage. "And just to be clear, when I pulled away from you out there, it was because you startled me. Not because it was *you* putting your hand on my arm. I *like* touching you. But I'm trying to be polite and cognizant of what *you* might be feeling. It's what good people do."

He grunted at the apology that had morphed into a heated admission of her unexpected attraction to him. "Red-haired temper?"

Her temperature rose as embarrassment flooded her cheeks. But there was something sparking in those pale gray eyes that made her realize he was amused by her inability to let any slight go unchallenged. Reese shook her head as her smile returned. "Wow. You change emotional gears faster than any man I've ever met. If we were old friends, I'd punch you in the arm for teasing me like that."

"We *are* old friends."

Reese frowned. "What do you mean? I thought you seemed familiar to me, but didn't we just meet this morning?"

He shook his head. "Dad directed you in *Annie*."

She'd been ten when the university had put out a casting call throughout Kansas City for youngsters to audition for the orphans and title role of the musical. Reese scrolled through her memories. "That was my first starring role."

"Didn't put it together until I saw you onstage earlier. You've got curves now you didn't have back then. Sang beautifully."

"Thanks."

Jackson shrugged. "A lot of annoying girls in that show."

Reese snapped her fingers as the memory surfaced. "That's right. I remember you now. The big, silent boy. Your dad brought you to rehearsal some nights. You'd sit out in the auditorium and do your homework. Or hang out in the light booth and play with the boards." Jackson was so much older, broader, and bearing the scars of a violent life now. No wonder she hadn't made the connection herself when she'd tracked him down at the crime lab. "I don't think you ever said a word to me. But I was kind of bratty and made myself at home with the whole theater. I sat down beside you one night during a break and went through your schoolbooks. You were reading *Hatchet* by Gary Paulsen." She had no trouble remembering him now. "You let me read it. I hope I thanked you for that."

Jackson nodded, indicating she had, and he pushed his elbow toward her. "You can punch my arm now."

Who knew this big, taciturn man had that wry sense of humor? She wondered how many people actually got to see that humor. Instead of punching the proffered arm, she wound her fingers as far around his warm forearm as they could reach and squeezed. "I am not hitting you. You were a nice boy then, and you're a nice man now, Jackson."

He grunted at the compliment, and Reese had to press her lips together to keep from laughing out loud at his go-to response when he didn't know what to say. She released his arm and headed toward the steel-and-concrete stairs that led to the storage loft. "I'll show you where I unloaded the box."

Once upstairs, Reese stood back while Jackson took pictures and sorted through the costumes and props that had been in the same box with the bloody knife. If she ever had to play a part that called for stoicism or intense focus that never missed a detail, she'd channel Jackson Dobbs. "I can't believe I didn't recognize you." He asked her to point out every item she'd touched, even the items she'd put in the trash. Plus, he scanned her fingerprints with an electronic device to eliminate her trace from the items he bagged and labeled. "You've changed a lot in twenty-three years, too. You're obviously taller, deeper voice, a lot more muscular."

"Uglier," he pointed out. "The Army and time in a boxing ring took a toll on me."

"You have an interesting face. A little beaten up by life, maybe, but interesting." She laughed. "Of course, I didn't notice boys back then the same way I do now. Back then, I only noticed the books they read."

There. His mouth quirked up at the corner and Reese beamed in return. She felt like she'd won a prize for earning that shadow smile.

He ushered her toward the stairs ahead of him.

"You turned me into a Gary Paulsen fan with that book. I've read the entire series since then."

Jackson offered no response, but she could still see the hint of his smile. As they came down, she noticed the stagecraft class had erected the interior walls and framed out the garden doors that would lead out onto the balcony of her set. She felt a little rush of excitement knowing that in the next day or two, they'd move the pieces to the main stage, and they could start setting lights and rehearsing with actual doors and windows. The plan was to have the set in place, if not with the finishing touches, by the Lowrys' open house at the theater this weekend.

But the thought of moving the set reminded her of all the cleaning and straightening up she'd been working on. "If that knife was used in your parents' murders, where has it been? That box hasn't been here for twenty-three years. Did the killer put it there, thinking they were getting rid of it? Did Beatrice Lowry take it from the killer, and has been protecting him all these years? Is someone trying to hurt the Lowrys? Will you investigate their family? The people who were at the university back then?" She crinkled up her nose as an unpleasant thought struck. "Will you investigate me?"

"Man."

Was she really learning to interpret what his terse responses meant? "A man killed your parents?"

He stepped down to the main floor beside her. "Man's strength to subdue my father. Depth of the wounds."

Compassion for him squeezed her heart. "How horrible to know things like that about people you love."

His icy eyes held hers for an endless moment before he gave her the slightest of nods. "Still have the box itself?"

If she knew him better, she'd have given him a hug. But she was learning that Jackson was like an animal that had been abused. He needed time to process his emotions and what he wanted to say, and he was cautious about his interactions with other people. She'd have to be patient about earning his trust and building a relationship with him—provided he wanted to be friends and spend more time with her outside his investigation.

The way she apparently wanted to. Reese turned away from him to hide her reaction to that surprising thought. Why was she even thinking about relationships with everything she had going on in her life? Maybe she was the one who should be more cautious about deepening her friendship with this man. In some ways, she felt as if she had known him twenty-three years. In others, she'd only known him for this one day.

"It's in the recycling dumpster. I didn't see any blood in it, though." She led the way out the back door. "But you might be able to get other information from it."

"Prints. Trace."

He held the door for her, and she pulled the front of her jacket together against the brisk autumn breeze. The sun was high in the sky. But there was a park and walkway that led down to a small bridge over a creek behind the theater. The tall pin oaks that were just starting to turn gold and the rich green pine trees cast long, cool shadows across the back of the building.

"It's like you're gathering all the pieces of a jigsaw puzzle. When you fit them together in the lab, it tells you the story of what happened. I love puzzles." She pulled a crate over to stand on so that she could reach into the bin to pull out the box he wanted. "This is it. I labeled the boxes once I opened them."

He shooed her hand away and retrieved it with his gloved fingers. He spared a few moments to examine it, then he pulled a large, flat paper sack from his kit and unfolded it. Reese held it open while he slid the flat box inside.

"Is that it?" She discovered she was reluctant to see him go. He was probably ready to carry his gear out to his truck or whatever Jackson-size vehicle he drove. "Do you need anything else?"

He pointed to his watch, giving her another look at those forearms. "Nearly two hours. You have class."

Wow. A man who truly listened to what she had to say. She was pleased that he paid attention to what she'd said earlier.

Despite her earlier caution to slow down whatever connections she was building with Jackson, Reese couldn't stop the smile that curved her lips. "I've enjoyed hanging out with you this morning. I'm glad you figured out how we knew each other. I hope you find something useful that can lead you to the answers you need about your parents."

"Not leaving yet."

That little rush of excitement she felt was unexpected and probably misplaced. "You're not?"

"My jacket?"

The hopeful feeling quickly crashed and burned. Jackson didn't want to spend more time with her. This was just good old-fashioned practicality. "Of course."

He opened the door for her, and they walked side by side back to her office.

"I don't suppose there's any way to tell if that knife was in that box for twenty-three years, or if someone hid it in there after it arrived at the theater." He shrugged. There was probably so much science behind the work he did that even a talkative man wouldn't have time to explain it all to her. "Can you figure that out at your lab?"

"Possibly."

"How? You study the other things that were in the box with it? The items you bagged as potential evidence?"

He nodded.

"Do you think…" She was flattered at how he gave her his full attention when she spoke. She was surrounded by college students who were consumed by their social lives and career goals, and fellow staff and supervisors who thought she was beneath them since she wasn't a fully accredited doctor with a PhD yet. She'd been ignored and talked down to throughout her life because of her age or her sex or her height or her youthful looks. Even if she received a terse or growly response, having Jackson Dobbs hanging on to her words, as if they had meaning and she was someone important, was good for her ego. "Is that the knife that killed your parents?"

"Can't say yet. Same type."

So, there was a possibility she'd uncovered an actual murder weapon. "Do you know if it was human blood on the blade and the blouse?"

He nodded. She shivered at the memory of what she'd given him. "That was a lot of blood."

He nodded again.

Reese pushed her key into the doorknob of her office. But instead of the key sliding into the lock, the entire door swung open. She froze in the doorway, a sick feeling curling in the pit of her stomach. Accidents happened, sure, but she swept her gaze across the office, anyway. She knew. Something was off.

Changed. Violated. "I swear I locked that. Maybe I didn't get it closed all the way."

But no such luck. There it sat, on the prop table. Another disturbing gift.

A syringe skewered a note into the wig and foam head.

Chapter Four

"Reese?"

She let the anger swell up before the fear could grab hold. "Oh, come on. Not another stupid joke. Coward." She muttered the word under her breath before stepping around Jackson and yelling into the backstage area to no one in particular. "Stay out of my stuff!"

Jackson put his arm out, blocking her path when she reached for the graphic message. "Don't touch."

Then he was pulling out his flashlight and fresh gloves again and studying the object she could barely look at. She yelped when she felt a hand at her back and spun around. "Damn it, Patrick."

The stagecraft professor quickly raised his hands up in apology. "Sorry, I didn't knock. The door was open."

Reese studied him from the receding points of his hairline down to the toes of his work boots before waving aside his apology. "No, I'm sorry. You startled me."

"Doing that a lot," Jackson observed from right behind her. His heat seeped into her body, and she didn't know whether to breathe easier or inch away. Once he seemed assured that she was okay with her visitor, he went back to work.

Patrick Brown flicked his short blond ponytail behind his shoulder, eyeing Jackson. "Everything okay in here? I heard you yell."

"I'm fine." Reese reached out to squeeze his arm to reassure him, and couldn't help but notice that she didn't react to his veins and muscles with that same rush of awareness she had with Jackson. "Someone was in my office. Has your class been backstage with you the whole time?"

"Up until I dismissed them a few minutes ago. Most of them went out the back door, but a few crossed the stage. Exited through the lobby, I suppose."

"Did you loan any of them your master key for the building?"

He nodded. "I asked a couple of boys to put some of the new tools away in my office. Until I can get another storage locker set up. I got it back, though." He pushed his glasses up onto the bridge of his nose and peered around her. "Another note?"

"Yeah." She stepped back so that he could see the syringe in the wig. Since Patrick had been with her that first night she'd found a message tucked underneath her windshield wiper, she couldn't very well hide the fact that her prankster had struck again.

"He's escalating if he's in your personal space." Patrick clasped her arms right above her elbows "You're not hurt, are you?"

"No. More pissed off. And a little rattled." She patted his hand before pulling away from his concerned touch. "I thought I locked my office."

"You did," Jackson said.

Good. She wasn't losing her mind or being careless. Someone else had seen her lock the door.

"I'm not the only one with a master key to this building," Patrick pointed out. "I keep telling Dean we need to change the locks after the vandalism incidents we've had. But he doesn't want the expense on this year's budget. I guess we have to wait until January to beef up security around here." He regarded Jackson warily, as if he thought he posed some kind of threat to her. "You want me to stay?"

"Jackson didn't do this. He's been with me the whole time. He's a friend." She glanced up at him, comparing the boy she remembered watching rehearsals with this mature, rough-featured man. What was wrong with people that they couldn't see him for the gentle giant he was? "I've known him for several years, in fact."

"Really? I haven't seen you around Reese before. Patrick Brown." The two men shook hands. "I'm chief set builder and supervise the tech classes. Reese and I go way back, too."

"Jackson Dobbs. Crime lab."

"You're Everett and Melora's boy. Dean mentioned you were on the premises." Patrick shrugged when Reese asked him when that conversation had happened. "That man gossips more than any old biddy I know. I think he wanted me to keep an eye on you."

"I'm fine with Jackson," Reese insisted. "Perfectly

fine. The dean probably wanted you to keep an eye on
why Jackson was here. He's paranoid about anything
getting in the way of the department's big launch
party with the Lowry family."

"Probably," Patrick agreed before turning his attention back to the larger man in the room. "I was a
senior here when your folks were killed. Your mother
tutored me so I could get through theater history and
literature classes." Patrick chuckled at the memory.
"I've always been better with my hands than I ever
was with words." Jackson grunted and Reese bit back
a grin. "Well, good luck with your investigation."
Patrick backed out the door, thumbing over his shoulder. "I'll be down in my office if you need anything,
Reese. Just holler. I'll come runnin'."

She followed her coworker to the door and waved
as he walked away. "I will. Thanks."

Jackson snapped a half dozen pictures before setting his camera aside. He carefully removed the syringe, studied what looked like condensation inside,
then dropped it into a hard plastic container. Reese
crossed her arms and leaned against the doorframe.
"What are you doing? This isn't a crime scene."

He opened his jar of black powder and knelt in
front of the doorknob. "Breaking and entering? Vandalism? Terroristic threats?" He continued to process
her office. "Tell me about the other *gifts*." He pointed
his brush toward her desk. "And that envelope."

Reese's shoulders deflated as she resigned herself
to getting someone else involved with her troubles.
"Some of the props we're using for the show have

been altered, damaged. The murder weapons, specifically." She pointed to the tray of broken glass, moving away as he pulled several prints. That had been the first gift after the notes started arriving. "One character dies by drinking poison. That tray was sitting on the middle of my desk when I came in after rehearsal one night. The bottle had been shattered, and the cranberry juice we use to mimic wine onstage had flooded the tray and soaked into my desk calendar blotter sitting underneath it. At first, I thought one of the stagehands had broken it and was afraid to fess up, so they left it in here anonymously. But there was a note under my windshield wiper in the parking lot that night." Jackson continued to snap pictures of the damage. "Another character is injected with a syringe. I'm afraid to see what shows up when they get to the character who's killed with an axe while chopping wood."

"Can you replace these?"

"Already working on it."

Wearing his sterile gloves, he bagged and labeled the abused props, and set them beside his kit. Then he straightened and nodded toward her desk. "The envelope?"

She pulled the manila envelope from beneath the pile where she'd tried to bury it and handed it to him. "They're distorted versions of the nursery rhyme that's used in the play. All of them are typed on plain white paper. None are signed." She watched a harsh line form between his eyebrows as he read them.

"The one on the wig is number four. I'm the only one who touched them, except for whoever left them. If they were dumb enough to leave prints." When he silently asked if he could take them, she nodded. "Each verse is supposed to be about one of ten little soldiers dying, just like in the updated version of the script. But someone has substituted nicknames for redheads in each one. They aren't in order. I don't know if that's significant, or if it just fits the messages they're sending me."

She was a quick study at memorizing lines. She didn't need to see the pages to know what he was reading.

Nine little freckle faces stayed up very late;
One overslept herself and then there were eight.

That had been the first message.

Then the culprit had gotten their hands on the props and added a more unsettling twist to each incident. The shattered liquor bottle had been the first.

Ten little carrottops went out to dine; One choked her little self and then there were nine.

The next incident had been her finding a copy of the script burning in an ashtray on the prop table. If she hadn't smelled the smoke after rehearsal and gone to investigate, the fire could have spread and done significant damage to the theater—or to her or anyone else who was there. Fortunately, she'd been able to put the small blaze out with her jug of water. But the message had been waiting for her under her office door.

Two red-hot mamas sitting in the sun; One got frizzled up and then there was one.

Now she could add getting stabbed with a syringe to the mix.

Six little fireballs playing with a hive; A bumblebee stung one and then there were five.

"These are what you mean by a joke?" Jackson asked. She nodded. "Not funny."

"Not to me." Still feeling a chill, Reese hugged her arms around herself. "I thought they might be fraternity pranks. Or messages from a disgruntled student because I won't let a theater class be an easy A for them. Or I didn't cast someone in the part they wanted. Maybe someone thinks it's funny that I'm directing a perfect murder mystery, and they're leaving me murder gifts that I can't figure out. I don't know. Maybe it's Maisey Sparks, trying to make me look incompetent or paranoid so that the dean will replace me with a director and professor she can manipulate."

Jackson was kneeling again, rearranging things in his kit to fit as many items as possible. "Someone's idea of courtship?"

"Like a student who has a crush on me? You mean

someone wants to date me, and thinks this is some sick way to woo me?"

"Woo?"

"People don't use that word anymore, do they?" Reese frowned. She couldn't think of anything more upsetting than being the object of someone's obsession. Again. Reese hadn't quit performing because of her parents' deaths. She'd quit striving for the spotlight because she hadn't been safe. The pedophile who'd targeted the pretty red-haired fourteen-year-old to be his plaything had been arrested, sentenced and subsequently murdered in a New York prison. "I suppose there could be someone out there who thinks if I get scared enough, I'd turn to them for comfort."

Jackson rose like a leviathan in front of her, forcing her to tilt her head. "Who would you turn to?"

Um, you?

But other than that wishful thought, the list was pretty short. Maybe a friend like Patrick. Although, one boring date had proved they would never be anything more than friends. Boyfriends had been few and far between with her work and school schedule and trust issues. With her father gone, she couldn't really think of anyone. "Maybe my brother-in-law? He's a sheriff's deputy in Grangeport."

"That's two hours away. Anyone here in KC?"

Reese forced a grin onto her face, determined to pull herself out of the pain of her past. "Is that your subtle way of asking if I'm available to go on a date with you?" She felt bad when a rosy blush tinged his angular cheekbones. *This guy isn't flirting! Just an-*

swer the question. "Sorry. There's no one. I… For all I know, you've got a girlfriend. Or a wife."

"Neither."

"Me, neither. I've been too busy getting my PhD and working to pay for it. I've always felt I have to work extra hard to get people to take me seriously."

"Why?"

"You really don't see it?" He frowned at the question. "Well, other than the fact there are still plenty of glass ceilings women have to break through in academia, look at me. I'm thirty-three years old. If you bound my breasts, I could still play Little Orphan Annie. Even with the boobs and hips, all some people see is the curly red hair and freckles. They see the wannabe child star who never quite made it—even though that hasn't been my dream for a long time. The people I want to impress always think I'm younger than I am. That I'm not serious about my craft or my job. That I don't have history. That I don't have secrets that wake me up in the middle of the night. That I haven't seen or been through things that make me able to empathize with others. I'm a grown woman. I've already lived more life than I ever thought I would." She shoved her fingers through her curly hair. "I thought about dyeing my hair a dark brown color and straightening it so I'd look older—"

"No." He reached for her hair as if he wanted to touch it, too. But he curled his hand with the crooked fingers into a fist and pulled away. "It's too pretty."

Whether he was remembering their conversation

about asking permission to touch, or he was self-conscious about his damaged fingers, she wished he'd been brave enough to run his fingers through her hair. "Dark hair would look horrible with my freckles, anyway. And those I can't change so easily."

He tucked his fingers into the front pockets of his jeans. "I'm judged by my looks, too," he stated quietly. "People have misconceptions."

Two full sentences of real empathy felt like a gift to Reese. "I imagine. At first glance, you're a big, scary dude. Well, at second glance, too," she teased. Did that quirk at the corner of his mouth qualify as a smile? "May I?" When she reached out to touch Jackson's arm beneath the rolled-up cuff of his sleeve, he nodded. Reese rested her hand lightly on his forearm, absorbing his heat, trying to ignore the little frissons of awareness that zinged across the sensitive skin of her palm. "But they're not looking closely enough. During the heat and humidity of a Missouri summer, I'd love to dive into an icy mountain lake the color of your eyes. These arms are quite… Hottie McHotterson. Clearly, you work out. And seriously, Jackson—you may look like a heavyweight prizefighter, but you've been nothing but gentle and kind with me."

"Not good with words." His shoulders lifted with a shrug, but she noticed that he kept his arm still beneath her touch, as if he was cognizant of possibly scaring her away.

Reese squeezed his forearm, proving that she wasn't afraid of the contact between them. "Not true. You may not use a lot of words, but you communicate just fine. With me. With anyone who pays attention. You have to communicate to work with your friends at the lab, right?" He nodded. "And Dean Diamant sure got your message."

He parted his lips to speak. Instead of producing words, though, he darted his gaze to the open doorway behind her.

"Yo, Ms. A. You coming to class or are we getting a free day? Whoa."

Reese startled for the umpteenth time that day. But Jackson was already moving and planting himself like a wall between her and the door. After bloody knives and veiled threats, she was more unsettled than she'd like to admit. With her hand pressed against her thumping heart, she stepped up beside Jackson to face one of the young men in her class.

"I'll be right there, Chris."

The young man glanced from her up to Jackson and back, then shrugged. "Ok."

He was almost to the stage before she realized that Jackson had extended his undamaged hand toward her. A protective gesture. One that told her student—or anyone else who popped into her office and startled her—that she wasn't alone, that she had a friend who was looking out for her. But by the time she'd noticed the caring overture and reached out to take it, he was already pulling away.

Did he think she had rejected him? Jackson Dobbs was confident and imposing in so many ways. What had happened to make him so gun-shy about putting the moves on her? And why couldn't she make him understand that she wasn't averse to him trying?

With the moment to make that connection and put him at ease having passed, Reese respected the distance he seemed to want and circled around him to her desk. She grabbed her bag from the bottom drawer, slid in her laptop and the flash drive she needed for the class's PowerPoint presentation on stage movement. "I enjoyed spending the morning with you, Jackson. Well, not for the reason you're here. I'm so sorry about your folks. I lost mine, too, but at least I know what happened to them." When he arched an eyebrow with a silent question, she took a cue from him and gave the briefest of synopses. "Car accident. Winter storm. Black ice."

She'd save the details of that heartbreaking night for another time. "It has been nice to get reacquainted and talk to…someone who listens." She turned the lock in the doorknob. "You see me doing this, right?"

He nodded.

"Just close the door behind you when you're finished. I'd better get going before my class runs off. Will you keep me posted if you find out anything about the knife or the pictures you took or…anything?"

Jackson nodded. "I'll look at these *gifts*, too. Whoever this is has to be watching you to know when to deliver them without being seen."

He was right. Whoever was pulling these disturbing pranks had to know her. This wasn't just about the skewed poem and props. "He knows when to call me, too."

"Explain."

"I've been getting mysterious phone calls," she admitted. "You know, when you answer and someone hangs up or no one's there?"

"Here or on your cell?" When she hesitated, he guessed the answer. "Both?"

She nodded. "My contact information is on the university website, so it's not hard to find me. They come within a few hours or so after each of the messages arrives."

"Late at night?"

Of course. Wait until she was alone and it was dark before adding to the torment. "I think he's checking my reaction to his latest gift. I'm assuming it's a guy, at any rate. His breathing sounds…male. He probably gets a thrill out of hearing my voice."

"Part of the game." Whatever game that might be.

"Knowing someone is there, but all you can hear is breathing or background noise? That's always creeped me out." Some of those nightmarish details of the accident were coming out, anyway. Why was it so easy to talk to this man? Was that a trick of not saying much? To get other people to fill up the quiet by pouring out conversation?

"When my parents were in the car wreck, they knew it was bad," she started. "Help wasn't coming in time. My mother called my sister at college. My father called me." Her eyes stung and she blinked back tears that wanted to fall. "I could hear Mom telling Reggie they loved her, loved us both. But it was already too late for Dad. He lost consciousness and succumbed to his injuries without saying a word— just the silence of a connected call. I could hear the wind, groans of pain. I listened to Mom breathing… until I couldn't hear her anymore, either." Man, she could use a hug right about now. But this quiet, cautious man wasn't offering. *Suck it up and get to the point.* "I have a good imagination. When no one's there, it makes me think something's wrong. Very wrong. Not my favorite thing." She swiped at the moisture in her eyes and forced some energy into her posture. "So, on that downer, if you ever call me, be sure to say hello. Don't sit there breathing and wait for me to start talking."

"I won't," he answered as if it was a solemn promise. He shrugged into his jacket and gathered an armful of evidence bags. "When are you done working tonight?"

"After rehearsal? It takes me about twenty to thirty minutes to make sure everything's put away and locked up. And all the students have gone, of course." Mostly likely, he just wanted a simple answer. "Ten o'clock? Ten thirty?"

He moved past her out the door. "See you then."

"Do you think you'll have some answers that quickly? More questions? Jackson?" But he was already striding away with his first armload of evidence bags. He was an enigma. But sweet and shy. Considerate. Protective. And more masculine than any man she'd ever met.

"Ms. A?"

Reese smiled and hurried out to the stage to meet her students. She wasn't sure if Jackson Dobbs had just asked her out on a date, had follow-up questions about the knife or was simply being chivalrous and worried about her safety. But she knew she was looking forward to later tonight.

Chapter Five

Jackson leaned back in the shadows behind the steering wheel of his truck, mentally debating whether he was doing his civic duty, being a creeper or hoping in vain that those sparks of interest he'd felt from Reese that morning were legit, and not a figment of his lonesome imagination.

Yes, he was doing his duty by keeping tabs on an old crime scene and potential witness. Yes, he was keeping an eye on the pranks surrounding Reese that history and his well-honed survival instincts told him might be merely scratching the surface of something much darker and more sinister. And he hated the idea that Reese was caught up in the middle of it.

Yep, he qualified as a creeper, too. The group of girls who filed out the back door of the theater, laughing and talking over each other, paused when they saw the big man lurking in his truck. They fell silent for a split second, then all chimed in again, trading warnings and making a beeline for the one car they all piled into before quickly driving away. Two more groups of college-aged men and women exited the

theater and either drove away or headed down the
path into the woods that cut through the park sepa-
rating the education buildings from the dormitories
on campus.

And yeah, he was sitting here in the dark of night
watching every single one of them.

He was watching and waiting for the curvy little
dynamo, whose petite stature belied the size of her
personality and the wattage of her smile.

Because spending time with Reese Atkinson was
an experience unlike any other he'd ever had with a
woman. Twenty-three years ago, when the cute and
bubbly star of the show sought him out and included
him in her circle of friends. And today, when a bold
woman approached him, not once but twice, defending him from the hurtful, mocking words he'd long
ago learned to let bounce off his tough hide. And
then telling him his eyes were soothing and saying
that the bulk and muscle that made him so intimidating made him—what had she called him? *Hottie
McHotterson?* Whatever those silly words meant,
he'd felt them inside like a breath of sunshine in his
dark, distrustful soul.

Yeah, he was cautious, but he wasn't stupid. He
liked Reese Atkinson. And he got the feeling she
liked him—at least as a friend. So, here he was, sitting alone in a parking lot at 10:15 p.m., ready to do
whatever was necessary to protect the first woman
who'd made him feel something in a very long time.

A single male student left the theater and headed
out along the path into the park. Although Jackson's

internal radar alerted with suspicion at the lone figure keeping to the shadows and disappearing among the trees, he stayed put. The guy was walking away, not looking over his shoulder to see if he was being watched. Another pair of students shot out the door and dashed down the path to join the young man. Jackson released the tense breath he'd been holding. Not a threat.

This morning, he'd justified his convoluted offer to meet Reese after rehearsal because she'd given him the first new lead anyone had had on his parents' murders in twenty-three years. Grayson Malone had identified three different blood types on the knife and blouse. Two of the blood smears belonged to his parents. But without fingerprints on the knife, or a sample to match the unknown blood donor to the killer, he wasn't much closer to finding the truth about his mother and father. He squeezed his hand into a fist and rubbed at the ache in his chest. He wanted answers, or a chunk of his life would always feel incomplete. He'd gone into this line of work to find the truth, to honor his parents and bring himself closure. He'd helped the crime lab and the KCPD solve plenty of crimes. But thus far, he'd let his parents down. He hadn't found the peace of mind he needed. He wanted to feel better.

Reese Atkinson's smiles made him feel better.

Her curly red hair and countless freckles that he wanted to explore with his good hand and taste with his lips filled him with a yearning anticipation that had him looking forward instead of staying trapped in his past.

She was caring and forthright in a way that was completely different from how he was raised after his parents' deaths. In Curtis Graham's house, there was no asking permission to touch someone. He'd either gotten yelled at or ignored, and never touched at all. In his uncle's house, affection was earned by achievement—and for a shy, grieving boy who was just trying to get from one day to the next, he had no hope of bonding with the family who'd taken him in. There was no hand-holding or hugs or easy smiles after his parents had passed. In the Army he hadn't expected hugs and softness, so he was never disappointed while he served his country. But in his personal life, he'd always hoped that he'd find unconditional love and support, the tenderness and laughter that he'd known with his mother and father.

Jackson was learning that he had friends among his coworkers at the crime lab—men and women he could depend on and sometimes socialize with. That's why he'd said yes when the lab's computer guru, Chelsea O'Brien, had asked him to be an usher at her wedding in November. Chelsea had given him a hug that day. The quirky, brainy coworker who'd survived an abusive childhood, and nearly died at the hands of a cyberstalker, loved to give hugs, and Jackson admitted he liked having friends who accepted him as he was.

But finding a woman? A family of his own? It was

hard to get his uncle's words out of his head sometimes: *Nobody wants you, boy. You've got to make
yourself somebody special before anybody's gonna
give a damn.*

Not that he thought any of this was a fairy tale,
and that Reese was going to magically fall in love
with him.

But he really, *really*, wanted to spend more time
in the aura of pretty smiles and positive energy that
was Reese Atkinson. He wanted a friend from his
past, from the good memories in his life. He wanted
new memories to savor, good feelings to blot out the
darkness of his life.

He intended to see that these pranks didn't snuff
out that aura and dim Reese's light. And he was damn
well going to make sure that the threats Reese had
received weren't a prelude to disaster, like the threats
his mother had received in the weeks before her murder.

Jackson silently cursed when the theater door
opened again, and a young couple walked out and
wound their arms around each other's waist. He immediately recognized the dark-haired young woman
who'd been so rude to Reese. Simon Lowry's granddaughter. Maisey Something—with a different last
name than the Lowry fortune. Beautiful in the way
of overly made-up fashion models and stylized por-
traits, but lacking any of the warmth and compassion
that oozed out of Reese's pores. The couple leaned
against an expensive purple sports car and started
making out.

Tired of being stuck with his own thoughts and feeling like a voyeur, Jackson heaved a resolute sigh and opened the door. The couple stopped and looked across the several parking spaces that separated them from Jackson as he climbed down out of his truck. Although the young man had the grace to look a little embarrassed to be caught with his hand under Maisey's shirt, the young woman herself narrowed her eyes and blew a mocking kiss at Jackson.

Whatever. He locked his truck, stuffed the keys in the pocket of his jacket and strode past them toward the theater's back door. He remembered from his parents' time here that the door would lock automatically, and could only be opened from the inside after hours. Still, he would be there, waiting to walk Reese safely to her car as soon as she came outside.

He heard two car doors close and one vehicle drive out of the parking lot. He was already turning at the crunch of gravel on the pavement when a car pulled up to the curb behind him.

Maisey rolled down the passenger-side window of her purple Porsche and yelled at Jackson from behind the wheel. "What are you doing here at my theater, Beast?" When his only reply was to arch an eyebrow at her juvenile attempt to belittle him, she laughed. "You really are Ms. A's boyfriend, hmm? Dean Diamant said you were related to that couple who got killed here. That you were reopening a murder investigation." She revved the engine, probably attempting to show him that she had power and money and could claim the dean as a friend. "Whatever you're up to, don't mess anything up for me. An agent and a producer from New York are coming to the season launch party and to see me in the play. My uncle and granddaddy tell me I'm going to be a star. But not if Ms. A gets in the way. Or you."

Jackson wondered if the young woman was a spoiled diva or extremely insecure, and if she had the means to back up her threats. Asking questions like that wasn't really his thing, but he had no chance to pursue any kind of conversation as she shifted the car into gear and sped away.

Alone once more, Jackson breathed in the cool autumn air and surveyed the parking lot again. The place was down to two vehicles. His truck and Reese's car. He'd asked Chelsea to get her license plate number so he could find it and park close by. He was glad to see her car right beneath a streetlight, but less pleased to see how far away from the theater she had parked if she had to walk that distance on her own. He heard no voices coming from the trees, and saw no one on the path, so those students must have made it back to their dorm rooms.

While the quiet and loneliness was relatively commonplace for him, it didn't sit right that Reese had to face the night or the threats or anything else on her own.

When he heard the click of the bar inside the door being pushed, Jackson swung around and grabbed the door. There she was, her shoulder sagging with the weight of her bag, her eyes looking tired and her short red curls stirring in the breeze.

"Any other incidents?" he asked, realizing a second too late that he hadn't given her room to clear the exit and make sure it was closed. He released the door and backed up a step at her startled gasp and inwardly cursed before tucking his fingers into the front pockets of his jeans to show that he wasn't a threat to her. This woman had a hair trigger when it came to surprises. A man looming over her when she stepped out the door was a big one. She wouldn't be the first woman he'd made uncomfortable by standing so close. And he sure didn't want to add to the stress she'd already had to deal with today. "Sorry."

"Hello to you, too." But she smiled up at him, and that told him he hadn't screwed up too badly. "Did you need to go back inside?" He shook his head and gestured toward their vehicles. "Just here to walk me to my car, kind sir?" Yeah, that smile did make him feel better. She checked to make sure the door was secure before grasping the straps of her quilted carryall and heading out. "Did you find out anything useful at the lab today?"

He wanted to offer to carry something for her. But she'd dinged him for that this morning. Besides, as heavy as the bag looked draped over her shoulder, the straps clutched in both hands, it was all she had. He settled for shortening his stride and falling into step beside her. "No prints on any of the notes."

They'd reached the parking area and stepped off the curb before she spoke again. "What about your parents?"

Grayson's report had been heartbreaking and given

him hope all at the same time. "Mom's and Dad's blood is on the blouse. Knife, too."

Reese halted. "Oh, Jackson. I'm so sorry."

He turned to see the stricken expression on her upturned face. "Grayson couldn't ID a third donor. Samples are too degraded."

"Who's Grayson?"

"Friend at the lab. Blood expert."

"But that confirms the knife was used to kill your parents? You can trace it to the owner or something? The third blood donor must be the killer? Please tell me finding that helps you."

Her eyes were a deep violet blue in the shadow he cast over her. He shifted to the side to let the harsh light from the streetlamp catch in them and make them sparkle again. Oh, hell. Those were tears glistening in her eyes. "I didn't mean to upset you."

"You're the one who should be upset." He watched a tear spill over and magnify the freckles on her cheek. "That's such a violent way to die. I'm sure they fought back. Maybe they even tried to save each other."

He rubbed at the weight pressing on his chest. He'd read the forensic details in the thin evidence file until he had the facts memorized. "Dad was attacked first. Mom may have been collateral damage. May have tried to intervene. But she was the one getting threats."

Jackson heard Reese's pained gasp, felt it deep inside himself, clenching around his heart. She reached up to cover his fist with her hand, and he stilled the habitual movement. "They must have loved each other so much. You were lucky to have them in your life for as long as you did. That's how I cope with losing my mom and dad—I remember all the wonderful times before they were gone." She slipped her fingers into the center of his fist and stroked his palm, easing his tight grip. "I suppose a man who deals with crime and death has a hard time thinking of the good things. Tell me a good memory about your mom and dad."

Jackson held himself perfectly still beneath her hand. Funny how even though her skin was cool to the touch, he felt something warm and bright seeping into his blood from the contact. With her touch, her patience, a flood of memories from his childhood filled his head. This woman must possess some kind of superpower. He couldn't not feel better when he was with her. He might as well share the most important memory. "They always called me their miracle boy. Mom had several miscarriages. I'm the only child she carried to term."

Another tear ran down her cheek and dripped off her chin, but she was smiling this time. "You were a treasure to them, I'm sure."

Jackson raised his other hand to wipe away the tears she was shedding for *his* loss. But he stopped himself before touching her. He didn't want to scare her away from this intimacy he was feeling.

Her gaze shifted to the hand he dropped back to his side. She sighed and pulled back, tugging the cuff of her blouse from beneath her jacket to dab at her empathetic tears. She headed toward her car again. "Were they robbed? Carjacked?"

Breaking contact was the opposite of what he wanted. He hurried after her. "Nothing taken."

"A crime of passion, then. Is that what it's called when the attacker loses it in a fit of rage, and goes after someone like that?"

Instead of agreeing or explaining the technical terminology used in their lab reports, Jackson asked. "Do you like pie?"

"What? Is that code…? Um…" She spouted a few partial sentences, looking confused by the question. "It's not my favorite dessert. I'm not a fan of mushy cooked fruit. Why?"

"When I have a bad day, I like to get pie. Pearl's Diner has the best. They're open late." He rambled on, not sure he was making sense. They crossed the last few steps to her car. "You're probably tired. I'll make sure you get inside safely, then you can go home."

"Does Pearl's have ice cream?" He felt her hand at his elbow as she stepped up beside him. "Could they make me a milkshake?" The soft smile on her full pink lips gave him a sliver of hope. "Ask me. If that's what you want."

She knew he was trying to ask her out? Trying and failing. But this beautiful, kind, insightful woman understood. He didn't think she was setting him up for a joke, either. That had happened once in the Army. He'd gone to a bar with some of his platoonmates and thought a woman there was coming on to him. Believing she'd been sincere in wanting to go home with him had been the punch line. While she laughed at his invitation with her friends, he'd gone back to the base and hammered a heavy bag without gloves until his knuckles started to bleed. But this was different. Reese was different. She hadn't done anything to make him think she was playing him. She was worth the risk, right?

Find the words to say what you mean. Spit 'em out. "Want to get a milkshake? With me?"

"I'd love to." The tension in him relaxed at her eager response. She reached up and touched her fingertip to the corner of his mouth. "I like it when you smile. I've had a tough day, too, and could use a little self-indulgence." He held the door to her car while she climbed inside. "I've never been to Pearl's. I've got GPS. But could I follow you and meet you there? Then we won't have to come back to campus."

And she'd have a means of leaving on her own if she discovered she wasn't comfortable with him. That had happened before, too.

Fifteen minutes later, Jackson locked his truck and jogged around the corner to meet Reese when she got out of her car. They'd hit the shift change at the KCPD and dinner break with the fire department. Being so close to the downtown stations, Pearl's Diner was a popular eatery for the city's first responders. The parking spaces in front of the diner were already taken, so they'd had to find spots the next block over. But Jackson wasn't worried about waiting in line. He and his team from the lab sometimes came here after working late on a crime scene, and he knew the servers and cooks at Pearl's kept things moving quickly with their simple, tasty food and reliable service.

Of course, tonight would be different, he thought, as they joined the line waiting to be seated. He probably wasn't scoring many points with the last-minute invitation. And if they had lousy service, he'd be scoring a big fat zero with Reese. Thankfully, she wasn't complaining.

"Two." Jackson held up two fingers when it was their turn to be seated.

The new server who greeted them at the door never looked him in the eye. The dark-haired woman whose name tag read Mollie glanced at Jackson's chest, maybe raised her gaze up to his chin, then focused her attention squarely on Reese. "This way, please."

Jackson didn't take it personally that she was skittish around him. A lot of people were wary of his size and tough-guy looks. But he suspected there was something more at work here when she walked a wide berth around the tables where only men were sitting. Even the ones where some Kansas City's police officers sat. Was she leery of cops? Or men in general?

"Hey! Mollie, is it?" When an older uniformed customer grabbed her wrist, she literally shied away and bumped into the table across from him. "We need more coffee."

Jackson instinctively touched her elbow to help her gain her balance, and she jerked away again.

"Sorry," she muttered to the front of his jacket. "Sorry," she apologized to the table she'd bumped, causing their drinks to slosh over the sides of their glasses. She immediately pulled a cloth from the belt of her apron and mopped up the mess. "I'll bring refills."

"Good golly, Miss Mollie," the older man who'd grabbed her teased. "How hard can it be to bring a coffeepot around and refill our mugs?"

The waitress cleared her throat and glanced at the impatient customer. "I'll be back as soon as I scat this couple."

"The longer it takes, the smaller your tip."

"Dude. Lighten up." A dark-haired uniformed cop spoke from the table on the other side of the booth divider. "Let her get her feet under her before you become *that* customer the staff gossips about back in the kitchen. She's new and they're obviously slammed tonight."

"Mind your own business, Standage. The little lady and I have reached an understanding. Right, babe?"

More interesting than her reaction to Officer Grabby Hands was that the waitress's eyes locked on to the police officer standing up for her. Those two knew each other.

"Hey," the officer greeted her. Jackson had met

Joel Standage when they'd both been part of a murder investigation the previous year. He didn't know Standage well, but he'd gotten a sense that he was good guy.

Still, Mollie looked like she was about to bolt. Even as Jackson moved to position himself between the waitress and her rude customer, Reese stepped up beside the woman and smiled. "Hey. Everything okay? Ignore him. He's not going to do anything stupid with us and your friend across the way around. Where do you want us to sit?"

"He's not my friend. I thought I recognized him. But the man I knew is dead." Mollie tucked a long strand of hair back into her ponytail. "It's fine. I'm fine. Sorry. Come this way." She moved a little faster when she saw how close Jackson was following behind her. But Officer Grabby Hands wasn't going to touch her again. Jackson exchanged a nod with Officer Standage. She seated them at a booth in the corner. She waited for him to slide into the seat across from Reese. She spoke straight to Reese. "Water?"

"Please."

Jackson didn't take offense. Mollie wasn't the first woman to be cautious around him.

"The menus are there on the table. Unless you already know what you want?"

Reese looked across the table at him, then up to the waitress again. "Excuse me."

When Reese grabbed her purse and slipped out of the booth, Jackson assumed she was headed for the ladies' room. Or maybe to say a few choice words to

Officer Grabby Hands. Or maybe he was completely wrong about her, and she was rethinking agreeing to this impromptu date and was leaving him.

Chapter Six

The last thing Jackson expected was for Reese to circle to his side of the table and scoot into the seat beside him. She wasn't running away. She was moving closer. Her thigh brushed against his.

Reese reached for his hand between them and laced her fingers together with his before lifting them to rest on top of the table. She was holding on to him in plain view of the waitress and anyone else in the diner to see. Although the top of that curly red hair barely reached his shoulder as she sat beside him, she had taken control of the situation here. Her ease with being close to him put Mollie at ease. Her words even elicited a shy smile from the waitress. "I've heard you make a pretty mean milkshake here at Pearl's."

Mollie nodded. "The menu only lists chocolate, strawberry and vanilla. But since we make ice cream sundaes, too, we can basically create any flavor you want. I like to swirl in an extra shot of syrup. Whipped cream and a cherry, too, if you want."

"You're my kind of woman. Butterscotch?"

"Sure."

"That sounds yummy. I'll take a butterscotch milk-shake. No cherry. But yes to the whipped cream. And my date here—" she glanced at Jackson and squeezed his hand "—would like to know what kind of pie you have."

Date. She'd called him her date.

Yeah, everything felt better when Reese Atkinson was around. Jackson breathed easier and felt the urge to smile. He couldn't even complain that she was holding on to his mangled hand.

"Since it's so late, we don't have everything. But you have a few choices." Mollie listed off the flavors they had left, and Jackson ordered caramel apple.

She was making eye contact with him now. "Warmed up? À la mode?"

"Both," Jackson answered. "And coffee."

Mollie smiled. She'd deemed him safe, thanks to the way Reese acted around him. At least he was less of a threat than the jerk who needed a caffeine fix and a lesson in manners. "Just made a fresh pot. I'll get those right out." She brought them water and coffee, poured a cup for the handsy customer, then headed behind the counter to fix their desserts.

"This *is* a great place." Reese scanned the diner, taking in every detail from the wall-to-wall windows at the front to the black-and-white tiled floor to the soda fountain, complete with red vinyl stools. "I love the kitschy decor. Seems to be a popular place for first responders. No wonder they're open late. They're doing a booming business."

"She was afraid of me. Afraid of every man in

here. But she relaxed. Because of you." Jackson looked over his bulky shoulder into Reese's upturned face. "You're good with people."

She shrugged off the compliment. "Nah. That guy was a jerk. I just offered her a means to escape. It's a woman thing. Like when there's no toilet paper in the stall and you ask a complete stranger in the one next to you to loan you some, they do it. Women help each other out."

Jackson had no idea what that reference to unified female pride meant, but he wasn't going to let her downplay her gift. "You're a star in the theater, on and off the stage. But I think your way with people is your real talent."

She shrugged. "I was just keeping the peace. It stopped you from knocking that jerk's block off. You're scary when you go into protector mode like that. I swear you were suddenly six inches taller when you stepped between Mollie and that guy. You did that at the theater, too, with Dean Diamant. Made *me* take a step back, and you were defending me."

"Reese." He held her gaze and made sure she saw he was serious about the rare gift she had that he could never hope to master. "Take the compliment."

Her freckles disappeared beneath a blush. "Okay. I did a good thing. I helped Mollie feel better herself, and about you. And I defused the tension in the room. Thank you for noticing." He waited for her to release his hand, but she never did, and since he liked the feel of her soft bejeweled fingers laced with his, he made no move to let her go. "It comes from necessity, I suppose. My sister and I have always had to stand up for ourselves. Battling the insurance company, lawyers, creeps in courtrooms, employers, directors, students—"

"Dean Diamant?"

"Him, too. I don't know if I'm an extrovert so much as I'm good at playing one. All my experience in the theater has given me the training to pretend to be whoever I need to be." After a few seconds of silence, she turned their hands over and studied his misshapen fingers. "What happened to your hand? Is it rude to ask?"

He shook his head. "I was a boxer in the Army. Still hit the gym to work out. Repetitive injury. Scar tissue on the bones."

"They don't impact the work you do now?" He shook his head and wiggled his fingers for her. They were stiff, but functioned. She lifted her other hand to trace the crooked arc of his pinkie and ring finger. "Do they hurt?"

Not when she caressed them like that. "The first couple of times I broke them, yeah. They work. They'll never be straight. They'll develop arthritis one day. I can already tell when rain or cold weather is coming."

"Ouch." She sat beside him for several long moments, fiddling with the silver and turquoise rings she wore, adjusting the man's watch that circled her wrist, checking the time. He wondered if she was considering letting go of his hand and moving back to the other side of the booth. She surprised him when she closed both hands around his. "Can I tell you something?"

He waited for her to continue.

She understood that was a yes. "I'm glad you came back tonight. To the theater. That place is creepy at night. Even if you don't believe in ghosts."

"Something happen?" In the one day they'd gotten reacquainted, he knew it wasn't like her to hesitate like this. "Come on, Freckles. You've told me everything else today. Don't stop now."

She suddenly lightened up and chuckled. "Freckles? Really?"

He touched several of the pale pink marks on her hand. "It's like you've been sprinkled with fairy dust."

"They make me look like I'm twelve years old."

His gaze dropped to her full unadorned lips, then boldly skimmed the generous curve of her breasts and the shadow of cleavage between them, curious to know if those freckles went all the way down there, too. Then he lifted his gaze back to the unique violet blue in her eyes. "No man would ever mistake you for a twelve-year-old."

She blushed beautifully and Jackson felt the need to kiss her, to lean down and claim her lips and show her in whatever rough-edged, but honest way he could muster that he had never met another woman who fired up his body, got him out of his brooding thoughts and cracked through the walls of his heart the way she did. Before he could act on the impulse to any degree, Reese pulled her hands away from his. Mollie arrived with their desserts, and Reese tasted a spoonful of her milkshake before raving to the waitress about how deliciously perfect it was with the butterscotch syrup swirled through it.

Jackson took his cue from her and stabbed into his pie, savoring the warm, spicy aroma before tucking a big bite into his mouth. Yes, it was delicious, and certainly gave him pleasure. But he'd rather be holding Reese's hand and sharing more conversation with her.

They ate for a few minutes in silence. Jackson polished off his pie before Reese spoke again. "You're not like any man I've ever met," she said, easing his fears about voicing his attraction to her.

He sipped the hot, strong coffee, keeping his hands busy so he wouldn't reach for her. "That good or bad?"

"It's…intriguing. You don't say much. Sometimes, I feel like you're searching for the right word or worrying too much about how people will react to you. And then, out of the blue, you spout poetry like the fairy dust. I think, maybe, you need to stay in the moment more—not worry about your past or try to foretell the future. I like the things you do say."

Right. His style was about as smooth as that crass cop who'd put his hands on the waitress. He steered the conversation back to a more work-related topic he could handle. "The theater was creepy tonight?"

"I've been spooked by weird stuff all day—dwelling on what all of it means." She set aside the last of her milkshake and finally got to the heart of the problem she'd skimmed over earlier. "You said your mother received threats before she was killed? What about?"

Oh, hell no. He wasn't ready to talk about this with her, was he?

"A grunt is not an answer."

He wasn't even aware that he'd made the noise. But since he'd already acknowledged his concern for Reese's safety, and could see a pattern repeating itself twenty-three years after the fact, he could hardly avoid letting her know the truth. "Love letters, at first. Then not so loving. All anonymous, like yours."

"Do you think whoever sent those letters is the man who killed your mom and dad?"

Jackson set his mug down and looked at her pale expression. Oh, hell. Did she think the messages she'd received meant someone would try to kill her, too?

She looked completely earnest as her hands fisted on the table. "I want to help with your investigation. There are…secrets at that theater. Old ones, new ones. As much as I love it, I'm not comfortable there. I made a mistake of going out with one of the professors—Patrick Brown, the guy with the blond ponytail and glasses?"

Jackson nodded. He remembered Brown, both from today, and from when he'd come to the house for Jackson's mom to tutor him. Twenty-three years ago, Brown's hair had been longer, and he hadn't started balding yet.

"I could tell after one night I just wanted to be friends. But he keeps pushing. My play goes up in two weeks, but props are being destroyed. I have to get everything ready for the Lowrys' reception. I get the feeling that Maisey is trying to get rid of me, and

Dean Diamant uses me as his verbal whipping post. It's like…"

"The spotlight's on you?"

She nodded. "I used to love the spotlight. All I wanted to do was act on Broadway."

"You were good enough." He sensed this conversation was taking a turn into difficult territory for her. Without thinking it through, he reached for her hand and held it gently against his thigh. Thankfully, she accepted that small bit of comfort and didn't pull away.

"Turns out, the price of fame wasn't worth the dreams I had."

"What price? This morning you said that secrets wake you up at night. A few minutes ago, you mentioned 'creeps in courtrooms.' Now you tell me you're spooked?" He hunched down to look her straight in the eye. "I need you to always be straightforward with me. Subtext isn't my best thing."

"Okay." Her grip pulsed within his. "I'm scared. Every time I get a note or busted-up prop, I get a sick feeling of déjà vu. I was targeted once before. It started when I was twelve. Just starting my career in New York. There was this man. He was obsessed with sweet little Reese with the big voice. He wanted to…marry me. He sent notes, flowers, gifts—came to every performance. He'd show up at my dressing room backstage. Restraining orders didn't stop him. He just changed his tactics to get to me." She paused and shivered. "When I was fourteen, he tried to kidnap me. He said he was going to make me his wife, and do things to me that fourteen-year-old me didn't even understand."

"*Tried* to kidnap you? Honey, if he took you for any length of time, you were kidnapped." How was Reese so...good? When crap like that had happened to her? Since she didn't seem to notice the endearment that had slipped out, he didn't draw attention to it by apologizing. But he did make a point of easing the anger from his grip before accidentally crushing her hand. "What happened?"

"My parents were rock stars. They saw me get dragged inside the van. Mom called in the license plate and description of the van while Dad jumped in the car and followed us. NYPD stopped the van with a spike strip, got me out and arrested the guy." She was shivering again. But her skin felt feverish, not cold. "I wasn't his first obsession. He had a record."

Creeps in courtrooms. "You testified against him."

She nodded. "Mom and Dad died coming home from his sentencing hearing."

First thing tomorrow, he'd ask Chelsea to dig up the court transcripts to get a name and location on this guy. "Is he sending the messages now?"

She shook her head. "Child molester? He was killed in prison."

Good. Not that Jackson condoned murder. But he wouldn't excuse anyone that evil getting close to Reese, either.

Turning toward him in the booth, she pulled back her shoulders and tilted her chin, like she was about to make an announcement. Jackson braced, fairly certain he wasn't going to like where this conversation was leading.

"I'm a grown-up now. I don't need Mommy and Daddy to save me. I'm not going to let anything like that happen again. Not to me. Not to one of my students. Not to my theater." Her hand pulled against his with every point she made. "The messages? Finding a real murder weapon? It's no secret that I'm the one in charge of the building. I think someone put that knife there for me to find. The dean ordered me to take care of those donations. The Lowry family sent them. How did I get stuck in the middle of all this? If I'm being targeted again, I intend to fight back. For my parents. For those girls before me who weren't so lucky dealing with that creep who took me. If I help you—asking questions, putting you in touch with some of the people who were involved with the theater when your parents were there—it would give me some control back. Make me less afraid. I'd feel less isolated if I knew I was part of a team that was searching for the truth."

"I'm a scientist, not a cop."

"I'm just asking questions. Keeping my eyes open. Reporting to you so you can do your science thing and come up with answers we can share with the police."

"Twenty-three years is a long time to get away with murder. He thinks he's smarter than us. Could be dangerous."

She waved her hand in front of him, sweeping from shoulder to shoulder. "You were in the Army. You box. You're built like a truck. I think you're a lot smarter than most people would ever guess. I have a feeling you're well equipped to keep me safe."

He repeated his objection. "I don't like you in danger."

"Jackson, except for my sister, I have been on my own since I was a teenager. I've dealt with being taken for granted, being laughed at, being underestimated and being alone." She pressed her fist to the tabletop. "I'm tired of *dealing*. I want to fight back. I think someone wants you and KCPD to reopen the investigation into your parents' murders. Maybe the killer has been hiding the truth for twenty-three years, and wants to finally be rid of the guilt. Or an accomplice who knows what happened has finally decided to break their silence."

"Maybe someone wants to kill again. Kill you."

"Maybe it doesn't have a damn thing to do with me, and I'm the unluckiest woman in the world to get stuck between a stalker *and* a killer." She released him to wrap both hands around his forearm, pleading with him. "But I'm not going to just sit here and do nothing. I'm a fighter. Like you. Maybe I don't have the external scars to prove it like you do, but they're there. Please let me help. You can be the brains behind the scenes, and I can be the mouthpiece on the front line."

"No."

She let go and turned away. "Great. I thought you were different. But you're dismissing me just like everybody else. You don't think I can get the job done. All I'm good for is looking cute and smiling."

"No."

"Would you please say something besides no? Tell me what you mean."

"No, you are not putting yourself in danger on the front line of this investigation."

"Oh." Spelling out his concern seemed to give her hope. "So, you don't mind me helping—you just don't want me to get hurt?"

He nodded.

"I can work with that." Her energy renewed, she dug into her bottomless pit of a bag and came up with a pen and small notepad. "Who would you like to talk to? What can I do to help?" She was listing ideas before he made any suggestions. "I can get you in to the Lowrys' party on Saturday. You could be my date. A lot of the people who were part of campus life twenty-three years ago will be there. All the people who have a grudge against me—that I know of—will be there, too."

"No one would believe we're a couple."

"Dean Diamant did. Mollie does. Do you have a tux?"

He didn't. "You'd go without me?"

"I have to be there, no matter what. Use of the theater is my responsibility."

"Then I'll find one."

"Thank you. I'll text you the details." She jotted a note with his name in it before snapping the pad shut and stuffing everything back into her bag. "I like that we've got another date planned. I'm sure I can help."

Although she could certainly ask questions of people who probably wouldn't talk to him, Jackson wasn't so sure her contribution would be worth the risk she'd be taking. "I want to meet you after rehearsals. Sit in on some. I don't want you alone late at night."

"That's good. Anyone who sees us would expect my boyfriend to pick me up."

"No. I want to make sure you're safe."

"Even better."

"I'm not acting."

"Neither am I." She beamed a smile up at him that lit the darkest corners of his soul. "Thank you for hearing me out. And giving me a chance to help fight my own battle."

Jackson paid the bill and left a generous tip before putting on his jacket and walking Reese out the door. He stuck his hands into his pockets so he wouldn't forget this was a first date and didn't do something stupid like act on that kiss he'd fantasized about.

"Look. You said you don't do subtext. I'm guessing you don't have a lot of good experiences with dating. So, let me make this clear." She hooked her hand through the crook of his elbow and stopped him. Then she slipped one hand into his and hugged herself around his arm, tilting her head back to make eye contact. "I'm interested in you."

"Why?"

"A bunch of different reasons. You listen when I talk. You don't dismiss me as inconsequential. You're protective. You don't care about the freckles or the extra pounds—"

"I like the freckles. And the curves."

"You like to read. I do, too. These arms. Some reasons I can't even put into words." Suddenly, her smile vanished, and she pulled away. "Are you interested in me?"

"God, yes."

She laughed with such relief that he smiled. "Good. I want to get to know you better. I want to spend time with you. You okay with that?" He nodded. She linked her fingers with his again and they headed down the sidewalk to her car. "All right, then. I'll be patient. And you keep trying to come out of that shell of yours. It makes me feel special to know that you're making the effort to do that for me."

When they rounded the corner and Jackson saw her squarish little toaster car, he halted.

"What?" Reese followed the direction of his gaze, then cursed and hurried forward before he could stop her. She went out into the street, circling around her car, taking in the damage. "What the hell?"

All four of her tires had been slashed, and two words had been keyed into the driver's side door.

Next time.

"*Next time* what? He'll give me a full-blown heart attack?" Reese demanded. Jackson followed her into the street and put up a hand to warn the approaching traffic to drive around them. She charged ahead of him before he could guide her back to the safety of the sidewalk. "I'm getting one of those cops from the diner." He nearly plowed into her when she suddenly stopped and turned. "Wait. You don't think this was that cop we stood up to for Mollie, do you? Maybe this is something different. Spur-of-the-moment rage. Everything else has happened on campus. And there's no clever message."

Jackson snagged her by the shoulders to stop her from moving away from him again. "There's a damn message. *Next time* he'll hurt you and not your car? *Next time* he'll kill you?"

Yeah. She got the message now. And he felt like a heel for driving the point home.

Reese nodded before twisting away to dig her phone out of her purse. "This has gone too far. I can't dismiss it as a prank anymore. I'm reporting it to the police." She pulled out her phone to punch in 911.

But Jackson already had his out of his pocket, speed-dialing his friend at the KCPD, Aiden Murphy. "Murph? I need a unit at Pearl's Diner right now. Somebody's after a friend of mine." Yes, it was the cute little redhead from this morning. And no, she wasn't hurt. "She's pissed, but fine. Now, Murph."

Once he knew that Aiden and his K-9 partner, Blue, were on their way, along with a priority call to Dispatch to get a black-and-white here even sooner, Jackson scanned up and down the street, peering around the glare of streetlamps and headlights, searching for anyone in the shadows who was watching Reese right now. He noticed she, too, was visually tracking every pedestrian, squinting to see faces inside the cars that drove past.

"This guy is good," Reese bit out between clenched teeth. "I've never seen him. Not once. Why don't you show yourself?" Her shout was drowned out by a car racing past.

Her phone rang in her hand. Her outburst of frustrated anger and fear fizzled out on the second ring. She must have thought it was the guy. She'd said he called her after every incident.

Jackson read the caller ID. Unknown. "On speaker," he ordered, leaning in to listen as she answered.

"Hello?"

Jackson heard someone breathing. Angry huffs of air. A sniffle as if a hard run in the cold air was affecting his sinuses. Then one guttural, ghostly word.

"Mine."

When her cheeks went pale and her hand started to drop, he grabbed the phone and put it to his ear. "Who is this?"

The abrupt disconnect echoed in his ear.

"Jackson?" Reese stepped toward him. "Put your arms around me."

Her whole body was shaking against his as he wrapped her up in his embrace and dipped his lips to the crown of her hair. The woman had a death grip on his shirt beneath his jacket, her lush curves pressing against his harder angles as she clung to him. With her face buried against his chest, he couldn't tell if she was sobbing with fear or shaking with anger.

In these moments when Reese had turned to him for comfort, something inside Jackson changed. The threat to Reese woke the warrior inside him. His heart might get shattered at the end of all this when she discovered she no longer needed him. But for now, this woman was his to protect.

She needed him. Needed his strength. Needed his heat. Needed him to hear her words. Needed him to stand tall and do the job he was trained to do. Find answers.

He squeezed her to his chest as tightly as he dared with one arm and raised his phone with the other. "Lexi? Jackson." He'd never been one for pleasantries. He was even less so now that he'd seen firsthand how these threats could hurt the woman he was falling for far too quickly. "I need Chelsea to trace a call for me. And send the team to Pearl's Diner."

Chapter Seven

The man waited until all but the police officer with the dog had left the scene before pulling the top of his hoodie over his head and sliding his hands into his pockets. No one would notice him dressed like this. He moseyed down the sidewalk away from the diner, right along with the curious lookie-loos who'd grown tired of watching the KCPD's response to his handiwork.

The CSIU van was still there, as well as a tow truck and a group of criminalists wearing CSI vests and jackets. They'd taken dozens of pictures and dusted for prints they would never find. One of them had even knelt in front of the message he'd scratched and pressed something like flypaper over it before peeling it off. Probably checking for any kind of trace that would indicate the weapon he'd used.

He ran his thumb over the pocketknife with the etched ivory handle that could only be found in antique stores or on the black market anymore. Typically, he preferred a bigger knife, but he hadn't planned on leaving a message for Red tonight. He was just watching her the way he did many nights. The way he liked to do with his women.

He'd never had a redhead before.

But he'd gotten so damn angry. Reese Atkinson was proving to be a handful of trouble. Sticking her nose into things that were none of her business. Refusing every chance he gave her to comply with his wishes. Being scared, but not scared enough to confide in him. Instead, she'd allied herself with that hulking shadow from her past.

"Big mistake, Red."

He reached his vehicle parked much farther down the street and climbed inside. He picked up his binoculars from the passenger seat and raised them to study the activity around her car. The tow truck driver was loading her ugly little eco car onto the platform at the back of his truck. He let his gaze slide over to the man in the leather jacket who was blocking his view of Red. She liked to collect ugly things.

The man in the car huffed with an angry breath. He needed to cool the fire heating his blood. He watched as Red stepped forward to shake hands with a man walking on a pair of crutches. Just as quickly, she drew back beside Mr. Ugly. Her posture flagged and she looked forlornly over at her car and waved goodbye.

Now he was getting through to her. He was the master of this game. And she'd be the prize when he won.

But the jolly scarred giant could be a problem.

He slipped earlier when he'd spoken on the phone.

She could have recognized his voice. Hell, that ape she'd turned to for comfort might have recognized his voice if his memory was any good.

He understood objectively that he had a sickness. That his way of pursuing a relationship wasn't healthy. But the heart wanted what it wanted.

And he wanted Reese Atkinson.

But there she was, hugging her heavy breasts around the big bruiser's arm as she clung to his hand. She'd gone out with him on a date, practically sat in his lap in the diner.

Red had found the knife he'd used on his beloved Melora. Mel hadn't done what he'd asked of her, either. Melora had been an accident. She'd been his first, but she hadn't been his last. He thought the evidence had been disposed of years ago, but he'd been betrayed. He should be doing all he could to cover his tracks. All he could to find out if someone had accidentally exposed him by sending the knife to the theater—or if the revelation had been done intentionally. But his compulsion ran too deep.

He lowered the binoculars and carefully stowed them in their case and tucked that into the glove box before starting his vehicle.

If Red kept working with the crime lab and the police, he'd probably have to kill her as soon as he took her. Usually, he could scare them into obeying him. For a while, at least. But then they either rebelled or surrendered, and he'd have to dispose of them and start anew. He had a feeling Red would be the kind to fight him every step of the way. But she would be tamed. She would obey him—even if it was only for a few moments before she took her last breath.

But he'd have to get the new boyfriend out of the way. Distract him if he could. Kill him if he couldn't. The behemoth shouldn't be touching what was his.

The figure sitting in the dark shadows of the parked car pounded the steering wheel with his fist. "She's mine."

JACKSON RAISED HIS head from the microscope where he'd been analyzing the trace Shane Duvall had taken from the door of Reese's car last night. He blinked to clear his vision, then pinched the bridge of his nose between his thumb and forefinger to alleviate the tension gathering there after an afternoon spent studying metal dust, identifying its components via chemical analysis, then evaluating each extracted component. It was time-consuming, painstaking work, and normally, he appreciated extended quiet time alone in the lab.

But this was evidence from the attack on Reese's car, and he was struggling to find his patience. The anonymous coward waging a terror campaign against Reese had escalated last night. Cool and calculating and hiding in the shadows to torment her was dangerous enough. Losing his temper to the point of lashing out at her and actually speaking on the phone was a whole new kind of threat. Unpredictable. Violent. There was no mistaking the rage he'd vented on her car last night.

Next time he might not stop with carving up her car.

If Reese had been anywhere near that guy last night... If he had taken that rage out on her instead of her property...? It was far too easy to imagine Reese's body disfigured by cuts and stab wounds lying in a pool of her own blood. He'd been to enough crime scenes, had taken enough molds of wound tracks, and had dissected and analyzed enough weapons to know what each and every wound would look like.

Jackson curled his hands into the meaty fists he'd once used to take down opponents in the ring and let his own anger course through him. He couldn't lose Reese. Hell, he'd barely found her. He hadn't even kissed her yet, and he had an idea that his life would be incomplete if he never got the opportunity to feel her beautiful mouth beneath his. He liked holding her hand. Loved how she'd gently caressed his broken fingers as if he was something precious instead of a fighting machine or a reclusive monster or a beast.

Put your arms around me. Last night when she'd been shaken up by her stalker's violent attack, he'd needed to hold her. To feel her softness against him. To feel her clinging to him as if she never wanted to let go. He'd almost hauled her up against him before she'd spoken. He needed to hold her to know she was safe and that the threats hadn't broken her beautiful spirit. She'd needed him. She'd needed *him*.

It was a heady discovery that filled him with a new kind of confidence where second-guessing had no place to dwell, where Uncle Curtis's voice and the harsh mantra that said he wasn't good enough to matter to anyone couldn't reach. Hearing Reese say she was interested in him wreaked havoc on all the bad memories that had taught him he was unattractive, worthless, not special enough for any woman to want.

Being with Reese Atkinson made him feel like the victorious boxer again. The valued Army sergeant on patrol with his platoon. The miracle boy his parents had loved.

He was going to hold Reese again.

He was going to kiss her.

He was going to find out who wanted her to be afraid.

Even more important than solving his parents' murders was identifying who was terrorizing Reese. He'd been a child when his parents had been killed. Even if he'd been on campus with them that night, he wouldn't have been able to stop the attack. But he was a grown-ass man now. He was a skilled criminalist, an Army vet and a champion amateur boxer. He'd see Reese safe, and justice served, or he'd die trying.

Jackson opened his hands and exhaled a breath to steady his focus, just as surely as a sniper would calm any movement of their body before taking a kill shot. Then he looked into the microscope again to confirm his findings.

He had a lead.

Nodding, he turned away to type the results into his computer. Then he sent a text to Chelsea in her computer lab with info on a search for her to run.

He heard a knock on the door and looked up as his friends and coworkers Grayson Malone, team leader Lexi Callahan-Murphy, Zoe Stockmann and Shane Duvall strolled in. Clearly, like Jackson, they'd finished running their tests for the day and were in wrap-up mode, unless the team got called to another crime scene.

Grayson pulled out a stool on the opposite side of the stainless steel table where Jackson was working. "Find anything new about the scene we processed outside Pearl's Diner last night? The prints I ran all came back to you or Professor Atkinson."

"You took charge of the scene and put us through our paces." Zoe was the youngest on the team. And, though she was the daughter of the veteran police officer who oversaw the CSIU and liaised with the KCPD, she'd more than earned her position as a solid criminalist. "I don't think I've ever heard you talk so much at one time."

"Exactly." Lexi gently elbowed the younger woman. "I think this sudden explosion of social interaction has something to do with Professor Atkinson. I like her."

Jackson grunted his agreement, then remembered Reese telling him that a grunt was not an answer. He was never going to be verbose, but he had words. "Me, too."

"Obviously." Lexi winked and pulled up a stool beside Grayson.

Great. This impromptu staff meeting was about to turn into an inquisition into his newfound interest in Reese if he didn't steer the conversation back to business. He nodded to Shane Duvall, a single dad whose beard and glasses made him look more like a professor than Reese did. "I processed the trace you took from the carving in the door. Good idea."

Shane grinned at what passed for high praise from Jackson. "Did you find something, big guy?"

"Minute paint chips and steel shavings from the car itself." Jackson moved the sample over to the projector scope and adjusted the image on the screen so he could point out his discovery to everyone. "But I also found evidence of bronze dust in the deepest groove of the *N* in *Next*."

"There's no bronze in a car chassis, is there?" Zoe asked.

"None at all." The director of the crime lab, Mac Taylor, walked in. "I wondered where my best team had wandered off to. Didn't realize I had called a staff meeting." He went up to the projection and adjusted his glasses to study the image with his one good eye. He'd been blinded in the other eye by an explosion at the old crime lab years before Jackson had come to work for them in this new facility. "You think you can identify the weapon from some dust? I know you're good, but…"

"Not precisely." Jackson did, as Reese had said last night, like to read. As the lab's weapons expert, he'd studied everything from a club made from the branch of a tree to jousting equipment, and from laser scalpels to military assault rifles, along with almost every type of gun or blade in between. "It's nothing modern. Probably from turn of the last century. Bronze is stronger than the iron originally used to forge the earliest of sharp weapons. But it's not as

strong as the steel used today. Bronze loses its edge
faster and needs to be sharpened more often. I'm
guessing the blade itself is misshapen from so many
years of honing. Some flecks from the last sharpen-
ing stayed in some of the pits or nicks on the blade
and were transferred to Reese's car."

"Can we identify the make of knife, at least?" Mac
asked.

Jackson nodded. "Based on the depth of the marks
and composition of the blade, I'd say we're looking
for an antique pocketknife."

Grayson propped his crutches against the edge
of the table. "An antique? You said the Bowie knife
from the theater that I processed had some age on it.
Are we looking for a perp who collects rare knives?"

"That's what I'd like to know." Chelsea O'Brien,
soon-to-be Buckner, came into the lab hugging her
laptop and a file folder to her chest. She set both on
the end of the table and fired up her computer. "I
need more search parameters to narrow down your
request for antique-knife collectors. I had no idea
there were so many knife shows and enthusiasts out
there. The Nelson-Atkins Museum has an extensive
collection of bronze weaponry. Not much that's as
small as a pocketknife, though."

Great. Jackson's lab was turning into a damn party.
But, for once, he found he didn't mind being the center of the team's gab sessions, where they hashed out
ideas and brainstormed solutions to their scientific
queries. Maybe because he knew they were there to
help him help Reese. Or maybe because Reese had

reminded him that he was as human and valued as anyone else.

She reminded him that he had a voice, and encouraged him to say what he needed to. "This guy isn't stealing them. We'd have reports from museums and vendors. We're looking for a private collector."

"That helps. Kansas City area?" Chelsea asked.

"Yes. This guy is local." He'd have to be to have such regular access to Reese, and to know the area well enough to remain undetected.

Chelsea typed the information into her laptop and started another search before handing him the folder she'd brought in. "Oh, and I've got the scoop on the guy who called your friend last night."

While Jackson skimmed through the data she'd collected, Chelsea explained what she'd found to everyone else. "I'm guessing Edwin Booth isn't his real name. I googled it and found a famous actor from the 1800s—the brother of John Wilkes Booth. I figured it was an alias since your friend works in the theater, and the other threats—"

"Focus, Chels," her friend Lexi reminded her. "We need the facts, not a history lesson."

"Right. Edwin, or whoever he is, paid cash for the phone. He used it the one time last night, and it hasn't been active at all today. Reese—I can call her Reese, can't I? Since she's your friend?" Jackson nodded, and she continued. "At any rate, Reese gave me permission to check her phone records. All the creepy calls that match the time stamps she gave me have come from prepaid disposable phones. Your perp used a different number each time. But the phones came from the same batch that was purchased two years ago." She shoved her sparkly cat-eye glasses up onto the bridge of her nose and frowned an apology to everyone in the room. "Unfortunately, the store doesn't keep security footage from that far back. So, I can't give you a visual on whoever purchased them."

Shane frowned right back. "I thought anything that was digitized on the web stayed there forever?"

"The store has a closed-circuit system on their own network." Chelsea wore an expression that said she was entirely innocent, but still so brilliant no one in the room would understand what she was talking about "I could hack into the store's system. But two years of overwriting the same security footage could lead to a pretty degraded recording, if any readable images still exist. If they were simply deleted, I could try to recover them, but it would take me some time to get a picture of your guy."

"And a court order," Mac reminded her. "Private property."

She turned her earnest hazel eyes to Jackson. "But if you ask, I'll do it."

Ask me. If that's what you want.

Jackson couldn't seem to keep his mind off Reese. The woman was a Jackson Whisperer, reading almost as much from the things he didn't say as the things he did. He was anxious to see her again. Eager to hold her hand—to hold her if she'd let him. And of all the longings he never expected to have, he wanted to talk to her some more.

He checked his watch. It might be close to quitting time here at the crime lab. But Reese would be at the theater until after rehearsal tonight. Ten o'clock seemed like a long time away. Maybe he could invite himself to a rehearsal. Or take her some dinner.

"Jackson?" Chelsea was still waiting for his answer.

He pulled his thoughts squarely back into the room. "Let's hold off on breaking any laws right now."

"Good call," Mac echoed.

"Probably," Chelsea agreed. "Buck will never forgive me if I'm in jail on our wedding." The others laughed. Chelsea picked up her laptop and headed for the door. "I'll get to work on finding your knife collector."

With his investigation into the man who was threatening Reese temporarily stalled until Chelsea got him some suspects with a knife he could compare to the marks on her car, Jackson asked, "Anybody know where I can get a tux in my size by Saturday?"

There was a squeal from the doorway, and Jackson looked up to see Chelsea making a beeline toward him. "You have a date? A fancy date?"

Jackson nodded. "Reception at Williams University."

Chelsea squealed again before coming around the table to hug him. "I really like Reese." Then she was opening her laptop again. "I'm going to find you that tuxedo right now. What size? Color?"

Mac tried to rein in the sudden flurry of questions and gaping mouths around the room. "Um, still work hours, people? Reports are all in? Equipment shut down? Evidence labeled and stored?"

Chelsea waved the boss aside. "My search is already running. This will take me two seconds." She turned her computer around and showed Jackson the map on her screen before clicking on one of the icons and opening an advertisement for him. "Here. There's a big-and-tall store down on the Plaza or at Barrywoods Mall in north KC. They have tuxes in stock. Take your pick. Nothing froufrouey for you. I'm thinking basic black. It's always classy."

Mac threw up his hands, but he was smiling as he stepped away. "On that note, I'm heading back to my office. If it helps, my wife and daughter tell me what color they're wearing before I pick out my tux. For the vest and tie or cummerbund."

"You have to call Reese, have a conversation with her," Lexi advised.

Jackson was flummoxed. "I have to wear a cummerbund? Hell, I didn't even go to senior prom. Look, I'm only going because some of the guests knew my parents and could be potential suspects in their murders. One of them could be targeting Reese now. I don't want her facing any of them on her own."

All the teasing suddenly grew serious. Lexi braced her elbows on the table and leaned toward him. "You think what's happening to Reese is the same thing that happened to your parents?"

Jackson nodded. "I think history may be repeating itself."

Now they were all back in investigative mode.

Chelsea was typing on her computer again. "I'll pull up any unsolved stabbings where the weapon was an antique of some kind."

Shane nodded. "A perp doesn't go twenty-three years between killings unless he's moved out of the area, is in prison or dead. Give me a list of suspect names and I can check where they've been in that time frame."

"Why do you think the two cases are related?" Lexi asked.

"For several weeks…before my parents were murdered…" Jackson hadn't talked about this until yesterday with Reese. "Mom got threats. Letters. Someone was stalking her, too."

"They're in the case file?" Lexi stood and urged Zoe and Chelsea to the door with her. "Let's pull the cold case file and read through the letters Melora Dobbs received. See if there are any linguistic similarities or production factors we can compare to Reese's."

"Or any unsolved cases Chelsea comes up with?" Zoe suggested.

"Good idea."

"What do you need from us?" Grayson asked. "You know I owe you for helping me when Allie was being stalked."

"You don't owe me anything for helping you save your fiancée," Jackson insisted. "She's good for you."

"Yes, she is." Grayson hooked the cuffs of his crutches onto his forearms and stood. "I'm helping you anyway. You need me to watch Reese's place? Pull bios on her students and coworkers?"

Shane headed toward the door. "I'll get busy running the tests to identify if that was poison or simple condensation in the syringe you retrieved from her office."

Jackson was a little overwhelmed by the support he was receiving. He mattered to these people. He might not have any of the Dobbses or Grahams in his life anymore, but he had *this* family. If he was lucky and didn't screw it up, he might have Reese in his life for a while, too.

"It's not a priority case for the crime lab. It's my case, my time. We have other crimes to solve."

"Does Reese mean something to you?" Grayson asked.

Jackson nodded. "I know it's happening fast. And maybe she doesn't feel the same way—"

"She wouldn't let go of you last night. Even when she was answering Lexi's and Aiden's questions and introducing herself to the rest of us, she kept her hand in yours or she had you in her line of sight. You mean something to her, too." Grayson adjusted his weight over his prosthetic legs. "It doesn't matter if it happens fast, or it takes years to recognize the connection you have to someone special. What matters is it happened. And if Reese Atkinson is important to you, then she's important to us. We're helping you find out who's after her and if it's related to your parents' murders."

"Thanks." Before his friend reached the door, Jackson stopped him. "Malone. How'd you know Allie was the woman for you?"

His friend turned and smiled. "She didn't put up with any crap from me. She got me out of my head, out of the pity party and anger I'd been living in since I lost my legs. But she still needed me. Not anybody else. Me." Grayson came back and rested a hand on Jackson's shoulder. "Tell me this—how do you feel when she holds your hand or smiles at you?"

"Better." Grayson waited for more of an answer. "Like my past and my scary looks don't matter."

"How do you feel when this guy sends a threat to Reese, damages her things, spies on her, claims her as his?"

"Like I want to rip his head off."

Grayson chuckled and smacked Jackson's shoulder. "It's not scientific. But I think we can safely say she's the one for you."

Chapter Eight

Reese ignored Dixon Lowry wiping his hands on his crisp white handkerchief again while his white-haired father, Simon Lowry, ran his fingers across the gritty oversize stone made by her student property master, Zach Oliver.

"This is papier-mâché and chicken wire, with actual bits of gravel dust incorporated into the finish?" The elder Lowry looked at the young Black man and congratulated him on the realism of his work. "Clever, son."

"Thank you, sir." While his gargoyle sat in Reese's office, waiting to be added to the display case in the lobby, Zach had taken great pains to produce a prop with the look and function they needed for the play. He also knew the importance of impressing their biggest supporter as Reese and Dean Diamant led the father and son duo on a tour to personally check out the venue for the Lowrys' season launch party.

Reese added her own congratulations. "Well done, Zach. This will look like the real thing onstage when we drop it on Inspector Blore. Sound effects, staging and his acting will make the audience believe he's being crushed and killed."

Zach's smile quickly faded when Dixon Lowry added his opinion. "Dad, the glue on that thing is still tacky. You have dust on your jacket already and you have dinner with the Vailes at seven." Dixon was a carbon copy of his septuagenarian father, except for the snow-white hair and the graciousness to others, no matter what their station in his life might be. "You'll have that thing put away before the reception, right? Our guests will be dressed to the nines. They won't want to get gravel goop on their clothes."

"It should be dry by tomorrow morning, sir," Zach apologized before Reese could stop him. "Then I'll move it out of the way to the prop table."

"You're making note of all the things that need to be fixed, Miss Atkinson, yes?" Dixon acknowledged Reese's presence without voicing any approval of the effort Zach had made in meeting both Reese's needs for the show and the scheduling requirements for the reception.

"Don't worry, Dix," the dean assured him. "I'll stay on top of Ms. Atkinson."

Reese clamped her lips down over her huffy sigh. "That's not necessary, Dean. Managing the theater is my job. Besides teaching classes, of course." She held up her notepad. "I have everything planned down to the last detail, and I have been in close contact with your staff and the student help I'll be working with."

Dixon put his hand on his father's elbow and turned him away from the worktable where the fake pediment sat up on two-by-fours to dry. "Come on, Dad. Let's move away from it before you get dirtier or hurt."

"My son thinks I'm old and infirm." The sweet man winked a rheumy blue eye at Reese. "I apologize for his rudeness. I'm enjoying the private tour."

Reese winked right back, thanking him for the apology. "Don't worry. Everything will be good to go Saturday night."

"I know it will." The older gentleman rubbed his hands together. "What's next?"

Reese gestured for Simon to follow her. "This way."

"Dad." It didn't seem right to hear a grown man in his fifties whining to his father. Apparently, the love for the theater that his parents and niece shared hadn't been handed down to Dixon. His custom-tailored suit and manicured nails seemed woefully out of place in this building where hard work and imagination created magic. But he'd promised his father that they'd personally check out the venue for the Lowrys' annual season launch party, so he reluctantly followed Reese and his father into the backstage area. "This is as clean as you can get it?"

Reese turned away to hide the roll of her eyes. This was Patrick Brown's construction area. Of course, there would be dust and sawdust, stacks of wood and cans of paint. She looked across a pair of sawhorses to meet Patrick's gaze and beg him to intervene with their guest.

With a nod to Reese, he stepped forward. "The set onstage is completely built except for the taping and touch-up painting. We'll have that done by the end of the day today so that everything is dry for the party Saturday night. I'll have my classes Friday sweep up and put things away so that our guests can tour the entire theater if they wish."

The dean tossed an arm around his friend's shoulder and guided him back toward the stage and auditorium. "Reese, tell Dix about the schedule for the evening."

Reese couldn't determine if the dean's presence on the tour was to check up on her performance in managing the theater, keep an eye on one of the school's biggest investors or seize the opportunity to catch up with a former fraternity brother from their student days at Williams U. Or maybe he was there for all three reasons. Regardless, she mouthed a thank-you to Patrick and fell into step behind the dean, Simon and Dixon.

Once they were back on the stage, Reese put her director skills to work to describe how the celebration would be staged. "We'll have food and drinks in the lobby, where faculty and students involved with the theater program will mingle with the guests to promote our upcoming season, and answer any questions about the shows, their classes and so on. Then we'll lead tours of the theater, except for the storage loft backstage and the catwalk where we hang the lights—for safety reasons, of course. If anyone wants to go up to the balcony and look in the light and sound booth, I'd be happy to show them that myself. Finally, we'll all gather in the auditorium for remarks from Dean Diamant and the Lowry family."

"And you, as well, dear." Simon Lowry touched her elbow and pointed a gently reprimanding finger at her. "You had a great impact on my late wife. She remembered you from the time you were a child appearing in *Annie*. And your production of *Twelve Angry Men* last season was the best drama she's seen on this stage."

Ignoring the glare Dr. Diamant was shooting her way from behind Simon's back, Reese blushed at the high praise. "Thank you, sir. Those are two of my favorite shows, as well—and very kind words. I appreciated all the support Mrs. Lowry gave to the theater."

"More than you know." Although she found the comment slightly cryptic, he smiled and patted her arm. "I sense that this place is as important to you as it was to her. Something like that is all you need to say."

"And the rest?" Dixon Lowry tapped his watch. Then he looked at Dean as if expecting him to take up his cause to end this meeting.

Take up the cause he did. The dean moved to divert Simon's attention. "Finally, we'll unveil the temporary sign built by our stagecraft students to commemorate Beatrice's generous donation—The Lowry Theater."

Reese's long hours, late nights and stress chose that moment to catch up with her, and she yawned. Although she quickly raised her hand to mask it, all of her company had seen it. "I'm sorry. I had a really late night. After rehearsal last night…my car was van-dalized. It was towed to the crime lab as evidence."

"Evidence?" Dean questioned.

"Yes. It could be related to…a case they're work-ing." Reese wasn't sure how much illegal activity swirling around her these past few weeks she wanted to share with the dean. No doubt he'd find some way to turn around the fact that she was the victim and blame her for bringing the authorities into his the-ater. "I had to hitch a ride to work with a friend this morning. But he needed to get to work early, so, not much sleep."

"Your friend, Melora Dobbs's son?" Dean asked. "The big guy?"

"Yes. Jackson. He drove me to campus this morn-ing."

"So, you two *are* close," the dean muttered, look-ing a little disappointed or frustrated or…some-thing…at confirming she and Jackson were more than acquaintances or childhood friends.

At least, she'd like to be close. Whatever was de-veloping between them seemed to be happening quickly. And though Reese wasn't averse to acting on this bond between them, she had a feeling that Jackson was a slow mover. Clearly, the man had his-tory that tainted the way he presented himself to the world. He'd been hurt or abused or shunned because of his looks and his shyness. She didn't want to risk scaring him away by pushing him too far out of his comfort zone before he was ready. On the other hand, every time she had pushed him yesterday—to talk more, to touch more—he seemed to welcome the encouragement, as if he'd been waiting for her permission to share more with her.

By the end of the night, she'd discovered he could be surprisingly bossy—both in his job and in the way he protected her. He'd introduced her to all his friends from the crime lab, then wouldn't let her anywhere near her car, even when one of them had asked her a question. He'd held her hand most of the time, or simply stood between her and the work they were doing. So, the alpha male that most women craved was in there. That just wasn't the part of his personality that he let show much. Until she'd needed his arms and heat to shelter her, and his expertise and take-charge demeanor to make her feel safe.

Jackson was plainspoken when he did have something to say, and he had been adamant that he would provide transportation for her while her car was at the crime lab. Her insurance would pay for a loaner once it was in the shop for repairs, but until then, he insisted on spending as much time watching over her as possible. Despite her argument that he didn't owe her around-the-clock protection, and wasn't responsible for her, he claimed that he had already dropped the ball twice by not preventing yesterday's events in her office and outside the diner. He wasn't going to let her get into a taxi or hired car by herself with a stranger when an obsessed stalker was terrorizing her for reasons they didn't yet know.

The man could be a shy poet. Or sweetly considerate. Or a scary guardian over whatever he chose to protect. She had a feeling he would be completely devoted to the woman he gave his heart to. He was appealing in so many ways. So yes, she wanted to say she was close to Jackson Dobbs.

"What's she talking about, Dean?" Dixon Lowry's barely whispered disbelief was hard to miss. "Her?" He glanced at Reese, then back at Dean. "The son of that man and woman who got murdered here? You know our families have history. *He's* dating her?"

History? What was he talking about? Had his parents known Everett and Melora Dobbs? Probably, since they'd been patrons of the theater even back then. "Do you know something about their deaths?" she asked, feigning innocent curiosity instead of pushing for information to help Jackson's investigation.

Smooth Dixon Lowry glared at her, as if she'd accused him of committing the crime himself. "No. Mom and Dad knew—what was his name? Jackson?—they knew his parents. Isn't that right, Dad?"

Simon nodded. "Yes, son. They were good people. Your mother and I worked with them often. Such a loss to the department and the university."

Dean smiled and turned their guests toward the front of the stage. "I think the point is that Ms. Atkinson had a rough night, with someone marking up her car."

"And slashing all my tires." Her unwanted fan had done a lot more than leave her a message last night.

Dean glanced back over his shoulder to her. "Are you all right? Were you hurt?"

"I'm fine." Dean Diamant had some acting skills of his own. His concern had sounded legit, even though she suspected it wasn't. He was probably showing himself as the benevolent boss in front of their guests. "Thanks for asking."

Dean shook his head and came over to her. "This isn't related to the other incidents, is it? Do we need to hire security for Saturday night?"

"I've already arranged for campus security to—"

Before she got the chance to explain that she was already being proactive about ensuring the safety of their guests, and that the threats seemed to be focused on her and no one else, Maisey Sparks pulled open the door of the theater and interrupted.

"Uncle Dix! Granddaddy!" Maisey swept down the aisle and up the stairs to the stage, where she hugged her uncle and traded kisses on the cheek. She embraced Simon, as well. Her smile became a sneer when she turned to Reese and dipped into her backpack to hold out a folder. "Here's my paper."

Dr. Diamant took the report and placed it into Reese's hands. "I'm sure you'll find it more than adequate to raise Miss Sparks's grade."

"I'm sure it will." She got his message loud and clear. *He* had done what was necessary to keep the Lowrys happy, whereas she had jeopardized the relationship by holding the young woman to the same standard she expected from all her students. She wasn't sure how much longer she could play the role of the dutiful underling for Dr. Diamant. "Dean, will you show our guests out?"

"Of course. Dix, why don't you come to my office, and we can go over the numbers of your family's donation."

Dixon winked at his old friend. "Got anything hidden in a desk drawer we can sip to warm me up? It's chilly in here."

"You know me too well. This way. Simon? Maisey? Would you like to join us?"

Invite an underage student to share a drink? Reese protested, "Dr. Diamant—"

"There will be plenty of time for you to have a drink to celebrate all your hard work after the reception on Saturday."

"I wasn't fishing for an invitation."

"Maisey, my girl." Simon crooked his elbow and held it out to his granddaughter. "Why don't you help an old man down these steps."

"Of course, Granddad." Maisey linked her arm through Simon's and led him down the stairs and up the aisle in the auditorium. "I'll show you to the dean's office."

Dixon let his father and niece reach the exit before he turned and extended his hand. "Thank you for your time today, Professor. I appreciate you coordinating with our family's caterer and decorator during this difficult time for us."

"I'm happy to help. I'm always proud to show off our theater."

Instead of releasing her hand, he tugged her a little closer, lowering his voice. "And don't worry. I'll keep Dean in line. I won't let him pour Maisey a nip of his whiskey."

Grateful that he understood her concern, Reese forgave him the uncomfortably long contact. "Thank you, sir."

"Dix, please."

"I'll see you Saturday, Dix."

"I'll be back to watch a little bit of rehearsal tonight. I enjoy seeing my niece onstage."

He lifted her hand and kissed it before jogging up the aisle to catch Dean and walk with him out the door. Reese fought the urge to wipe her hand on the side of her jeans. When he was getting his way, Dixon Lowry was all attentive charm like his father. But when he wasn't, the impatient, arrogant, faintly threatening Lowry came out. It explained a lot about Maisey's behavior if Dix was a role model for her. Reese didn't think that was charm so much as he was schmoozing someone he'd be working with this weekend. Or maybe someone he didn't want pondering his weird reaction to learning she was involved with Jackson Dobbs.

The moment the door closed behind her guests, Reese went back to her office. She was relieved to discover it was still locked when she inserted the key. She tossed Maisey's hastily written—possibly not by her—paper on top of her desk and picked up the scarf she'd been knitting for the play to unravel a few of the ends and tie them off with knots so it would look like a project in progress when used in the play. She completed two knots before sighing heavily and setting the prop aside. She circled her desk and sat down to look at Maisey's report. But that didn't hold her interest for long, either.

He's dating her?

Why did she find Dixon Lowry's angry whisper to Dean about her budding relationship with Jackson so condescending?

Our families have history.

What was it about two-thirds of the Lowry family she'd met with today that rubbed her the wrong way?

She shivered in her chair as if shaking off a bad memory. These past few weeks, she'd hated working in the theater almost as much as she had when she'd been the target of a sick man's obsession. She loved so much about the theater and teaching, but men like Dean Diamant and Dixon Lowry and whoever the hell was sending her those messages were ruining the creative life for her.

Maybe she should just move to Grangeport to live with her sister, Reggie, and her family. She could find a small-town businessman with simple goals to settle down with. Or a salt of the earth farmer and be his helpmate in an agrarian life. Of course, that would mean becoming a burden on her big sister again, at least temporarily. More importantly, it would mean giving up her dream of earning her PhD to honor her parents' sacrifice and proving to herself that the traumas of her childhood hadn't scarred her for life. Plus, she really was a city gal. And she wanted to see where this thing with Jackson might go.

Reese groaned aloud and reached for her phone.

Typically, when she was upset and needed a place to vent, she called her sister. But her thumbs were already pulling up Jackson's number and sending him a text.

Why are people mean?

She picked up Maisey's paper and started to read.
She'd only reached the end of the introductory paragraph when her phone dinged with a reply.

Another threat?

Reese smiled at that simplest of contact from Mr. Tall, Dark and Silent, and picked up her phone.

No. Just rude people.

Mere seconds passed while she waited for his reply. Instead of a message popping up, her phone rang. She smiled when she saw Jackson's number and answered immediately. "Hey."

"Hey, Reese. This is Jackson."

She giggled at his perfunctory announcement. "I know it's you. We were just texting, and I saw your number."

"You told me to always identify myself when I called."

She had confessed that unnerving little fear, hadn't she? "I know it's a hassle, but it's sweet that you remembered."

"It's not a hassle if it's something you need." Wow. She could fall in love with this guy if she weren't careful. "Who was mean to you?"

"Why? Are you going to beat him up for me?" she teased, needing to lighten up her thoughts and this conversation.

After a pause, Jackson's tone was dead serious. "Is that what you need me to do?"

Reese hastened to reassure him that she wasn't looking for more violence. "No. I don't want you to be an enforcer or my bodyguard. I just wanted to reach out to someone who…" *cares about me.* "Hearing your voice makes me feel better. I feel calmer about being here."

"Something did upset you. Are you safe? Alone?" He'd noticed her use of the word *calmer.*

"For now. There are a few people working backstage. My students will start showing up for rehearsal in a few minutes. I'm locked in my office, so don't worry. I just finished giving a tour to Dixon Lowry and Dean Diamant. Simon Lowry was here, too. He was quite charming. But he seemed tired. Still grieving for his wife, I'm sure."

"Lowry and Diamant know each other?"

"Yeah. Fraternity brothers from back in the day." She toed off her shoes and pulled her stockinged feet up onto the chair, hugging her arm around her knees. "Do you know Dixon Lowry, by any chance? He got weird when I said we were dating."

"Dating?"

"Yes." She pointed out what was obvious to her

in case it wasn't obvious to him. "We've had several long conversations, so we're really getting to know each other. You asked me out last night, and I asked you to the reception on Saturday. Those are dates. Hence, we're dating."

"Weird how?" he asked, without replying to her claim that they were a couple at the beginning of their relationship.

Reese shifted topics with him. She wondered if he had accepted her definition of their relationship, or if his idea of being interested in her was different from her idea of being interested in him. "I can't put my finger on it. He was pretty much bored and disinterested while I walked them through the details of Saturday's program. I suspect he was just there for his father's sake. Then Dr. Diamant said we were dating and he kind of panicked. Like he didn't want anyone named Dobbs to have anything to do with the theater, including me. So, you must know Dixon."

"No."

"Would he have known your parents?"

"Don't know."

Okay. So, if there was any connection there, it didn't mean anything to Jackson. Her suspicion radar must be working overtime, seeing clues and bad guys where none existed. "Then to top it all off, Maisey showed up to see her uncle and grandfather and tried to make me feel small."

"You're better than any one of them. Better than all of them put together." The pitch of his deep, gravelly voice dropped when he defended her. "Don't let them make you feel any less special than you are, Freckles."

Reese grinned at the silly endearment he used. "It makes me laugh when you call me that."

She could hear the cautious note in his voice when he said, "Is that all right?"

"Yes. Of course, you can have a pet name for me. It's another example of what people who are dating do." She lifted her gaze to the window of her office door as she heard footsteps and chatter coming from the stage. She was going to have to end this call soon. Then she eyed the new wig of gray wool she was knitting to replace the prop that had been skewered with the syringe, and had a sobering thought. "I just hope this creeper who's sending me messages doesn't use *Freckles* in one of his sick nursery rhymes. I don't want him to taint your nickname for me."

"We'll get this guy. We're developing a profile of the man we're looking for."

"You are? Can you tell me who I should be keeping an eye out for? Is there someone I can draw into a conversation at the reception to get you information? I already asked Dix if he knew anything about your mom and dad, and he just clammed up. He told Dr. Diamant that your parents and his family had history." Reese wrinkled up her nose at the memory. "Then he tried to be all charming and kissed my hand."

Jackson grunted.

"To be honest, it freaked me out after he'd been so put-upon by my tour, and then downright hostile. Like I said, weird."

"Don't confront anyone without me or the police there."

"We were in the middle of a conversation. It came up."

"Still…" Once again, he moved on to the next subject without explaining himself. "The police are looking for someone who's got enough money to be able to afford rare collectible knives—we're talking thousands of dollars or more. Either that, or someone who's really in debt because they're spending all their money on their collection. Or it could be someone older who has been collecting tools and weapons over several years."

Simon Lowry was older and wealthy. But that sweet gentleman had no reason to kill Jackson's parents. Dixon Lowry had the wealthy part down. And she did know someone with an extensive collection of every kind of tool under the sun.

"Patrick has more tools than any man I've ever known. In his office, in locked cabinets backstage, in his truck. Probably at home, too. I know he has a box cutter and a pocketknife. I'm not sure there are other weapons around here, except for props. And there will be several wealthy people here on Saturday. All our patrons are invited. I don't know if any of them are collectors."

Jackson grunted. What did that mean? Confusion? Disgust? Eagerness? She heard a screech of metal and wondered if he had pushed away a stool or chair he was sitting on. Judging by the even exhales of his breath, she imagined he was striding out of his lab or office.

"Jackson?"

"Is Brown there right now?"

She heard other voices in the background. Had he flagged down some of his friends at the lab?

"Yes. He's working in his office, I think."

He took a deep breath. The side conversation he was having with someone else faded away.

"Jackson? You stopped talking again."

"My friend Grayson is going to call campus police. They'll swing by the theater to keep an eye on things. Just in case."

She was a little frustrated and a lot worried. "Do you suspect Patrick?"

"You said he pressured you to go out with him."

"Yes, but I don't feel threatened by him. He's a friend."

She heard a knock on her door and looked up as Zach Oliver peeked through the glass and waved.

"I have to go. My students are arriving. You'll be here after rehearsal again, right? Or should I call a cab?"

"I'm driving you home."

She suspected he'd say that and felt relieved. "Okay." Zach knocked again. She lowered her feet to the floor and slipped on her shoes. "I'll be right there."

Zach pushed the door open and picked up several of the props they'd need for rehearsal. "The set looks cool, Ms. A."

"It does, doesn't it? You go ahead and start setting up the prop table. I'll be there in a sec."

He left with his props. Wait. How did he open the door if she'd locked it behind her? Reese hurried over to check it. Nope. The knob was still secure and wouldn't turn from the outside. It should have locked automatically behind her. She touched her finger to the latch that retracted and came out to seal the lock into the door jamb. It felt a little sticky, as if someone had taped it open. But there was no tape there now. She shook her head and turned back to her desk. Okay. Now she was creating mysteries where none existed. She probably hadn't pushed it all the way closed.

Reese forced herself to exhale the breath she'd been holding and slow the rapid drumbeat of her pulse. Zach had no reason to hurt her. And he hadn't even been alive when Jackson's parents had been killed. Her imagination was working overtime. "Jackson?"

"Still here."

"Will you say something nice to me before we hang up? Make me feel good about myself? Make me feel safe?"

The silence on the other end of the phone almost made her think he'd hung up. But she'd never heard a click. So, he was still there, listening. Reese was a little disappointed that he was too flustered or just didn't care enough to answer her request. "I'm sorry. I shouldn't have put you on the spot like that."

"I finished reading a new book. A thriller. I figured out the mystery, but it's still good." He shot the words out like a rapid-fire machine gun before taking a breath. "Would you like to borrow it?"

"Really? That's sweet. Bigger than a Gary Paulsen book, maybe, but just like old times. I'd like that." It would be interesting to see if his reading tastes had progressed the way hers had over the years.

"I'll bring it tonight."

She'd forgotten that this guy needed think time before he spoke. But every word he uttered was worth her patience. "You're making me smile so much right now my face hurts."

"Good. I love your smiles."

Love? No. He didn't mean what she'd heard. *Smiles, Professor. The man is talking about smiles.*

She picked up her director's notebook and headed for the door. "I really do need to go. I'll see you later."

"How many freckles do you have?" he asked from out of the blue, stopping her in her tracks.

"Um, I've never counted them. Why?"

"Are they everywhere?"

She could feel her face heat up. Her freckles were a bit of a lightning rod for her. Some men she dated seemed to work hard to overlook them. Others criticized them. One guy had even asked her to bleach them so she'd look more grown-up. "Why do you want to know?"

"Are they…under your clothes?"

The blush was still there, but confusion and wariness had given way to anticipation. "Are you flirting with me?"

"I'm trying. I haven't had a lot of practice—"

"All over." Uh-uh. She wasn't letting him back down from the most intimate thing he'd said to her yet. "From my forehead down to the tops of my feet. More so where the sun hits my skin, but all over." His groan deepened her smile. "Now you think about all those freckles, Mr. Dobbs, for the next two and a half hours while I'm in rehearsal."

"I will," he said matter-of-factly. "All of them."

"Jackson!"

"Do you feel good about yourself now?"

Delighted with his innuendo, she laughed. A sexy, overtly masculine man wanted to see her freckles, even the ones she hid from the world. How could she not be flattered by his words? "Yes. Much better. Thank you. I'll see you later."

"Count on it."

And that promise made her feel safe.

Chapter Nine

The good feelings of Jackson being silly and sweet and sexy with her didn't last past the second act of the play. Working with the actual set walls and platforms threw off some of the actors. The young man playing the judge had a meltdown because he was struggling to come up with lines he had recited perfectly the previous night.

Which set off Maisey into a whiny tirade about the unprofessionalism of actors making her look bad. Then Dixon Lowry had come to the front of the stage to comfort his niece, despite Reese's suspicion that the young woman was playing up the drama she wasn't really feeling in order to impress her uncle. And the moment she had started to question Maisey's sincerity, Dean had come down to defend Maisey and warn Reese that she needed to regain control of the rehearsal.

Reese had ordered everyone to take a ten-minute break before her redheaded temper spewed out of her mouth. After a private conversation to calm the young actor's nerves, and a reminder to Maisey that putting on a play was a team effort, and they should be supporting each other instead of tearing each other down, they made their way through the third act with the drama limited to the show onstage. The tension during the show's gripping ending was actually pretty darned believable, and she told the cast and crew that they were absolutely going to be ready for an audience the following week. She ignored Dean and Dix altogether, until she took her focus off the stage long enough to realize that both men had left the auditorium.

Reese checked her watch several times once rehearsal had ended, eager to see Jackson again. All things considered, she'd handled her stressors well tonight. But there was something inherently spooky about a cavernous auditorium that reflected every little noise, and a backstage area filled with props and set pieces that created creepy shadows. The actors quickly left. Patrick helped the backstage crew reset the stage for the beginning of the show before they all went home. Somewhere in between all that, the light booth and stage had gone dark, and the only illumination in the building were the security lights in the lobby and by the back door exit, along with the glow through the window of her office.

As theater manager, she made her usual rounds. She checked the timed locks on every external door to make sure they were secure, and then she focused on her own office door. She locked and shut it three separate times, convincing herself that the only way anyone could have gotten in was if they had a master key or they had sabotaged the lock. She'd make a point to ask Jackson about the sticky residue she'd felt on the lock. Then she closed the door and sat at her desk to grade Maisey's paper while she waited for Jackson to knock at the back door.

She finished the paper, quite certain that these weren't Maisey Sparks's words, and that they had been plagiarized or written by someone else. But without any evidence beyond her gut telling her that this wasn't how the spoiled student talked, and doubted she would come up with anything as insightful as twentieth-century drama being a metaphor for the social issues of the day, she debated whether it was worth confronting Maisey. With Dean Diamant and the Lowry name against her, Reese would have a difficult time proving her case. Although the university had a strict policy against plagiarism, it might be worth her own sanity to give Maisey the lowest passing grade possible and let her move on to be a terror in someone else's class.

And maybe that was a decision she needed to make after a little more research and a lot more sleep. She put a sticky note on the paper with the grade she wanted to give, along with a reminder to do an online search to find similar papers that had been published.

While she was straightening her desk and gathering her things into her bag, she heard voices, low and indistinct, coming from the auditorium. Great. Reese heaved a weary sigh. Had a couple of students hidden inside the building to make out or do their homework? Or they'd simply fallen asleep and hadn't realized rehearsal had ended.

It said Theater Manager on her door. It was her job to go out there and clear the building. She grabbed her keys and a flashlight, pulled the sweater she was wearing tighter around her torso and headed out the door. Although the backstage lights were in the opposite direction, she headed onto the stage. Her flashlight gave her path plenty of illumination. Besides, she had the ins and outs of this building memorized.

The voices were clearer out here. Not voices. One voice. "Oh, hell," Reese said.

Another prank. One of the sound effects used in the play was being broadcast from the light booth, where the sound controller also worked. It was the recording used onstage by the play's alleged killer that was meant to terrorize the guests in the production, and put them on alert that the murderer intended to kill them all for their crimes.

It was terrifying enough to hear that evenly modulated voice during the show. Hearing it now ticked her off, giving her more work when all she wanted to do was see Jackson and hopefully turn tonight into another date.

Reese marched off the front of the stage and up the aisle, shining her light into the balcony above her. "Hello? Is somebody up there? We're closed for the night. You need to go home." She pushed through the lobby doors and up the stairs to the balcony. "I don't know if you're trying to be funny, but this is an actual crime. Trespassing." She pulled out her phone. "I have campus police on speed dial."

When she unlocked the door to the light booth and saw the blinking lights of the soundboard piping the words into the loudspeaker, she realized it wasn't the recording from the play anymore.

It was her very own personalized poem of terror.

Ten little carrottops went out to dine; One choked her little self and then there were nine. Nine little freckle faces stayed up very late; One overslept herself and then there were eight. Seven hot little tomatoes chopping up sticks; One chopped herself in halves and then there were six.

Reese shivered and backed out the door. What the hell? She was alone, wasn't she? She'd said goodnight to the two young men who ran the lights and sound and watched them walk out the back door together. Maybe it was set on a timer. Computers could do that sort of thing, and all their sound effects were computerized.

But who? Why? What had she ever done to anybody except testify against a monster who was now dead, and refuse to play all of Maisey's and Dean Diamant's games to appease their egos? Was someone trying to scare her away from helping Jackson solve his parents' murders? But these pranks had started before she ever went to the crime lab to meet Jackson.

He'd said his mother had received threats before she was killed.

Was history repeating itself? Had she become the newest obsession of a man who'd gotten away with murder for twenty-three years?

Fear tried to squeeze common sense out of her head, tried to squeeze the bravery out of her heart. But she was stronger than this. This was a game to someone. And she wasn't about to lose any stupid mystery game.

Taking a fortifying breath, she stepped back into the light booth to shut off the vile recording...

And heard footsteps running across the catwalk where the lights were hung overhead. Her pulse hammered in her ears at the sound. There were two ways down off the catwalk—using a super tall extension ladder that was safely stowed backstage, and climbing down the ladder anchored to the wall of the light booth.

Reese slowly turned her gaze to the ladder just a few feet away that led up to the open trapdoor in the ceiling.

Open door. Ladder. Not alone.

"Get out," she whispered, willing her frozen feet to move. The footsteps were coming closer. "Get out. Get out. Get out."

Reese was running now. She slammed the door shut and raced for the stairs. She shoved open a lobby door and ran for the stage, with the cruel words still echoing throughout the theater. The footsteps she heard behind her could be the intruder coming after her. Could be the man running away. It could be her imagination. Could be nothing.

Reese didn't go to her office. She didn't grab her purse. She just ran. The beam of her flashlight found the exit and she pushed her unathletic body into a sprint. She crashed into the back door. Dropped her flashlight. Shoved it open, plowed into a man's chest and screamed.

The broad shoulders blotted out the light from the streetlamps. But then her panting breaths inhaled leather and soap and a scent that was already more familiar to her than her own perfume.

The moment she realized she was pounding on Jackson's chest, she stopped fighting and started grabbing. She crushed fistfuls of his jacket in her hands and pressed her body against his. When he didn't immediately fold his arms around her, she shoved her hands beneath his open jacket and clung to his shirt and the heat of the man underneath.

His hands lightly skimmed her shoulders. "Reese?"

"Just hold me."

Those twin bands of iron wound around her back, lifting her onto her toes as he snugged her tightly against his heat and strength. Reese uttered a noise that was half sob and half groan, like the pain and reviving warmth returning to frostbitten fingers. His fingers crept up to cup the nape of her neck and tunnel into her short curls. His lips grazed the crown of her hair. "Honey, you're shaking. What scared you?"

"Ask questions later. Just hold me a couple of minutes."

While his fierce hold on her never lessened, she was aware of him turning with her to prop his booted foot against the door, blocking it in case whoever was after her tried to come out behind her. "Was someone in there with you? I need to know how to protect you."

She shook her head and snuggled in, willing his strength and protection to chase away the panic and allow reasonable thought to return. Her lips moved against the hard swell of a pectoral muscle, while her pulse aligned itself to the steady drumbeat of his heart beneath her ear. "Another prank. I thought I was in there alone. But the sound effects from the light booth started playing. I went to check it out. Then I heard footsteps and I ran like some stupid damsel in distress." Now she was realizing she wasn't much of a detective or any help to Jackson's investigation. "Damn, I could have snapped a picture with my phone. I could have called campus security or the police. I could have done something useful. Instead, I totally spooked myself."

The fingers in her hair gently massaged her scalp. "Are you skilled in hand-to-hand combat?"

"No."

"Are you armed with a weapon?"

"Of course not."

Jackson leaned back against her arms around his waist and framed her face between his hands, tilting her face up to his. "Then you didn't do anything stupid. You did what was necessary to keep yourself safe."

The man was eminently practical, and that made

her feel better. She reached up to brush her fingertips across the scruff of his square chin. "Thank you."

She was shaking like a leaf on a brisk autumn wind, but she had something solid to cling to now. She could anchor herself to Jackson.

"You're still scared."

"Um, yeah. But I'll be fine. I'm better with you here—"

His lips dropped to hers and he was kissing her, consuming her. Jackson blew past the quick peck on the lips as first contact. He skipped the whole gently exploring, getting acquainted kiss. A fire kindled low in Reese's belly as his mouth blotted out all thoughts except for the sensual assault of his lips on hers. Jackson's kiss was as raw and potent as the man himself. She slipped her hand behind his neck to latch on to him even as his fingers pulsed against her scalp and kept her mouth pinned beneath his. She parted her lips to become a more active participant in the kiss. His tongue slipped in to tangle with hers and Reese groaned. Her breasts grew heavy, and the sensitive tips hardened into tight buds, which rubbed against his chest. She fisted her hands in his shirt and collar, holding on for dear life. The other women he'd dated must not have let him get to the kissing stage in their relationship, because they wouldn't have given up this toe-curling, panty-dampening ability to kiss. She wouldn't.

But all too soon Jackson tore his mouth from hers and straightened. Reese whimpered in disappointment at the loss.

"Are you okay?" he asked, his voice a gravelly rumble, his beautiful eyes dilated to the point she could barely see their icy gray color. His deep, harsh breaths seemed to match her own. She mutely nodded. "I didn't overstep?"

This time she shook her head from side to side, still in a daze over this man's secret talent. "I haven't been kissed in a while," she whispered. "I've never been kissed like that."

"Is the recording still playing?"

Recording. Reality. Reese squeezed her eyes shut and nodded, forcing her mind back to the danger that had sent her rushing into his arms in the first place. Wow. Jackson's kiss really was a secret weapon when it came to disrupting her thoughts. She hoped that kiss was about more than helping her move past her fears. But they could discuss it later.

She shifted her grip on Jackson to the more neutral location of the front of his jacket. "It's on a loop. I have to shut it off in the light booth. But you'll come with me, right?" He nodded. "The footsteps I heard were on the catwalk right above the light booth. Whoever was there is probably long gone."

He pried her hands from his jacket and tested the door before moving the foot that had been blocking it all this time. "You have keys to get in?"

Reese pulled her keys from her pocket and nodded.

"Let me get my kit from the truck. I'll check it out with you."

She felt chilled by Jackson's abrupt departure toward the parking lot. He had just turned her world upside down and set her heart on the path to falling in love with him. And now he was walking away?

But then she realized he'd only taken a few steps and was reaching back, his hand outstretched toward her, inviting her to take it. "Freckles?"

With a noisy sigh of relief at knowing he wasn't abandoning her, even for a moment, Reese hurried after him and slipped her hand into his. Jackson's grip tightened around hers and held on the entire time it took to retrieve his CSI kit and go back inside up to the light booth.

There was something extremely unsettling about a mechanical voice, listing off all the ways she could die, over and over. They paused outside the light booth long enough for Jackson to slip on a pair of sterile gloves and kneel down to study the doorknob.

"My prints should be on it," Reese said.

Jackson shook his head. "Wiped clean."

A chill rippled all the way down Reese's spine. "So, someone *was* here with me."

Jackson opened the door and visually swept the room before turning off the computer and silencing the voice. He removed the flash drive and studied it closely before dropping it into an evidence bag. He stretched his hand out to her again, and Reese didn't hesitate to take it. This time he pulled her right into his chest without her giving instructions or permission and held her close. He dropped his chin to the top of her head. "You aren't imagining this. The threat is real."

She nodded her thanks for believing her and settled against him. The embrace was brief as he had
work to do, but his support was enough for her to pull
away to share her observations and help him while
he inspected the sound and light boards. She pointed
to the trapdoor in the ceiling above them. "That was
open when I was in here before."

"I remember going up to the catwalk a few times
with Dad." He went to the ladder and started climbing. "Turn on the auditorium lights."

"It's okay for me to touch stuff?"

Jackson nodded. "This guy has wiped everything
clean. But he might not have been so careful up here."

Reese turned on the lights and watched Jackson
disappear through the door above her. A few minutes
later, the top half of his body reappeared through the
opening. "Get in my kit and hand me the small round
brush and the jar of black dusting powder."

She opened his CSI kit and climbed partway up
the ladder to hand him the items. "Did you find something?" she asked, before he shut the trapdoor over
her head. "I guess that's a yes," she muttered, climbing back down.

She startled when it opened up again. He pointed
to his kit. "I need a couple of those clear tape cards."

"Like you used in my office to pull up fingerprints?" He nodded and she quickly pulled the items
he needed and climbed the ladder to deliver them.
This time, she felt more curious than shut out when he
disappeared again. But only a couple of minutes later,

the trapdoor opened, and Jackson climbed down. "Did you find something useful?"

He held up two clear fingerprints. "As I suspected, he cleaned up down here, but neglected to wipe down the latch on the catwalk side."

Reese felt another shiver, but this was anticipation, not fear. "You can run those and find a match?"

"If he's in the system. Otherwise, I'll need warrants to obtain prints." He packed the items back in his kit, including the small evidence bag with the flash drive that held the recording inside. "I'll have Chelsea take a look at this. Maybe she can decrypt the data to find out where it was recorded. Or see if there are other files on it that will help her pinpoint the owner."

"Can she identify the voice, even though it was mechanically altered?"

"You didn't recognize it?"

Reese shook her head. "It's created like the sound effect we use in the play. But it doesn't sound quite like the man who recorded our message for us."

"Who was…?"

Her nightmare was about to become very real if the recordings were made by the same actor.

"Dr. Diamant."

Chapter Ten

Reese happily went with Jackson to the crime lab
to log the evidence he'd found. Although there was
a team on call around the clock to process crime
scenes, at night, the building itself felt like a modern, high-tech tomb. The floor-to-ceiling windows
in the main hallway reflected the interior lights and
blotted out the night outside. Jackson's office and
the lab she'd glimpsed gleamed shiny and sterile in
the bright lights. Jackson promised to bring her back
in the daytime to give her a full tour and reintro-
duce her to some of the friends he worked with. She
nodded at the invitation and gave an appropriate response about wanting to get to know the people who
were important to him.

But she was already thinking about what would
happen next. The man stalking her had promised
next time and claimed she was *mine*. Was scaring her
at the theater what he meant? Simply that he wasn't
done playing these games with her? Or was there
something more sinister waiting when he was done
tormenting her?

Then they were back in his truck, cruising through the lights and shadows of downtown traffic, heading toward her apartment complex. Jackson must have asked a question she didn't respond to because she felt his hand slide over hers and link them together on the center console.

"Freckles?" He squeezed her hand in his gentle grip. "You okay?"

"What?"

They stopped at a traffic light, and he turned to face her. "I asked if you wanted something to eat. You're a million miles away."

"I'm not hungry."

Rightly understanding that food wasn't at the forefront of her thoughts right now, he said, "Talk to me."

"He hasn't called yet. He always calls after one of these incidents." Reese turned to wrap both her hands around his. The colored lights from the dashboard and the darkness outside the car might have given Jackson's harsh angles and muscular bulk an ominous silhouette. But to Reese, there was something comforting about having all that solid strength to cling to. "Waiting for the other shoe to drop is giving me an ulcer. Maybe that's his grand plan. He wants to stress me out so much that I have a heart attack. Or I pass out, and then he can do whatever he wants to me."

Jackson grunted his displeasure at that possibility.

"And if he thinks all this is funny, that he's getting his jollies by watching me squirm and scream and cuss at him, then I want to punch his lights out. You can teach me how to do that, right?"

"You want me to teach you to box?"

"Maybe? I just want to be able to do something to fight back. It's not right to bully someone like this." She pointed a stern finger at him. "Don't you for one minute think that you are some kind of social misfit because you're not the handsomest guy in the room or the smoothest charmer. This guy is the misfit. He's sick. He's a coward. You're a real man. You stand up for what's right, for someone who needs you. I can talk to you. I like being with you. I trust you. I will take honest and shy over his kind of sick any day of the week."

He glanced behind him in the rearview mirror and pulled into the turn lane. Away from where she lived.

"Where are you going? My apartment is to the right. I'm venting too much. But I don't need pie or a milkshake."

"You shouldn't be alone."

"I'm not alone. I'm with you, thank goodness."

"I need sleep."

"Oh. Of course." Reese pulled her hand from his and hugged her arms around her bag in her lap. "I'm sorry. You don't have to babysit me. Just drop me off and make sure I'm locked up inside."

Jackson shook his head and turned the corner when the light changed. "He'll call when you're alone."

"Probably."

"You'll be afraid."

Duh. She let her frustration creep back into her tone. "Probably."

"I don't like it when you're afraid."

"Well, neither do I. But I'm a grown-up. I'm not Little Orphan Annie anymore. I'm not a child who needs her parents and big sister to take care of her. I can handle this."

"Stay with me."

"Huh?"

He glanced her way across the cab of the truck. "I won't force you to do anything."

"I didn't think you would. But Jackson, I'm already taking up too much of your time. You're not getting to work on your parents' murder case. Staying the night is a big step. We hardly know each other."

"Not true. I know you better than any woman I've ever met."

Even though she agreed that she knew him better than other guys she'd dated for months, she had to stop taking advantage of his good heart and penchant for standing up for her. "I know you're an introvert. Don't you need a break from me and all the chaos I bring into your world?"

"I can handle your chaos," he insisted. "We're dating. I don't want my…girlfriend…to be scared."

Oh, wow. There was so much to love about this man's plainspoken honesty. The urge to argue her point faded. "I'm your girlfriend?"

His eyes captured hers for a split second, but he didn't answer.

Reese repeated herself, but this time as a state-

ment rather than a question. "I'm your girlfriend."
She reached over the console to rest her hand on his
thigh and felt his muscles quiver beneath his jeans
at even that light touch. "I want to stay the night, if
you're sure. I don't want to be alone. I feel safe when
I'm with you."

Jackson dropped his right hand off the steering
wheel to lace his fingers with hers and hold her hand.
"I feel better when I know you're safe."

"I don't have any of my things," she pointed out.

"I have a new toothbrush you can use. I'm guessing one of my shirts will be big enough for you to
sleep in."

"Pretty sure." There'd be more than enough room.
And if his shirt carried his scent, she'd be surrounded
by him, guaranteed to sleep in comfort and have
sweet dreams—or erotic ones if she thought of his
body and those arms and that kiss.

They drove several more blocks in silence until he
steered his truck into a residential area. "Jackson?"

"Hmm?"

As much as the rawness in her settled at the security of staying with him, there was a different sort
of anticipation humming through her veins. "Since
I'm your girlfriend, will you be kissing me again the
way you did at the theater?"

He glanced at her with a hungry look, then turned
his focus back to the road. "You liked that?"

"No. I loved it. I don't think I've ever shared such
a grown-up kiss with a man before. It made all my

girlie parts stand up and cheer. And it touched something deep inside me. I've been alone most of my adult life, but I didn't feel alone then. I felt connected, like we were one, like that was how my life was supposed to be."

He frowned at her waxing poetic. "Girlie parts?"

"You do know what those are, right?"

He grunted. But the blush tingeing his cheekbones told her he knew exactly what she was talking about.

She continued to pour out her thoughts and praise him. "You, sir, have been holding out on the women of Kansas City. You've got skills."

"I haven't had that much practice. Just some casual encounters. Kissing wasn't really a necessity."

"Are you saying you're a natural talent?"

"Reese."

"Well, you can practice on me anytime." She squeezed his hand. "But not on anybody else. Because *we're* dating."

"I don't want to kiss anybody else."

"You need to stop saying sweet stuff like that. You're going to make me fall in love with you." The sudden stillness of Jackson's big body seemed to suck all the air out of the truck cab. *Dial it back a notch, Atkinson.* She had to remember that Jackson was a rare man who needed to move at his own pace. Reese smiled and tried to lighten the mood in the truck. "As long as you have a blanket and a pillow, I can sleep on the couch. I'm couch-sized."

He answered with a sound that was more than a grunt and almost a chuckle. "I have a guest room."

Good. She hadn't scared him away. Yet.

"Then I'm guest room–sized."

Their silly, intimate bantering eased the tight grip of fear inside her, and tempered the surprising depth of what she was feeling for this man. By the time they pulled up to a modest but well-maintained brick ranch, Reese was beginning to feel like this might be the ending of any other date with a man she'd stayed up far too late with.

Jackson warned her to stay put and climbed out of the truck first to check the neighboring houses and up and down the street for anything unusual before he opened the door for her, tucked her hand in his and led her inside. While she brushed her teeth and slipped on a gray Kansas City Chiefs T-shirt that hung to her knees, he checked the doors and windows of the house. Once he declared everything was secure, she sank into the double bed in the guest room and bade him good-night. Although she would have loved a good-night kiss, she was learning not to push. Jackson didn't believe how badly she wanted him yet. But he understood how much she needed him, and that was the feeling she'd cling to. He left her door slightly ajar and a night-light on in the bathroom across the hall before he retired to his own bedroom at the end of the hall.

She pulled the covers up to her chin and tucked her nose into the collar of his T-shirt. Yep. It had that clean masculine Jackson smell she was learning to crave. With a deep sigh, she turned onto her side and let the scent and security Jackson provided seep into her senses.

Reese was drifting off when her phone vibrated and lit up on the bedside table. That slight buzz in the night shocked her awake and she knew. It was him.

"No, no, no, no, no."

She pushed back the covers, swung her legs over the edge of the bed and sat up. The blinking light was garish in the slumberous cocoon of Jackson's house. She picked up the phone. Somehow the vibrations in her hand felt like his vile touch on her skin. Reese swiped the answer button and took a deep breath before speaking. "Hello?"

The labored breathing she hated brought tears to her eyes.

"I don't understand what you want. Why are you doing this to me?"

She yelped when her door swung open and Jackson's giant frame filled the doorway. She cowered away from him as he strode to the bed. "Hang up."

Since she was too shocked to immediately comply, he grabbed the phone from her hand and ended the call. Without hesitation, he turned off her phone and tossed it onto the bed, ending any chance of her stalker calling her again.

Reese's head was tipped all the way back to keep Jackson's grim expression in view. But his hand was gentle as he cradled the side of her neck and jaw and wiped away a tear with the pad of his thumb. "He made you cry."

She didn't know whether to nod at the obvious, or make a token stab at arguing she would be okay.

Jackson took the decision from her when he slipped his hands to her shoulders and pulled her to her feet. Then he was bending, curling an arm behind her knees and the other at her back, lifting her off the floor. She tumbled against his chest, coming to her senses enough to realize the man didn't sleep with a shirt on, and he was carrying her from the room.

Reese latched on to his shoulders. "What are you doing?"

"You're sleeping with me."

He seemed like a man who had made up his mind, and she wasn't a woman who wanted to protest his decision.

He laid her gently on his king-size bed and she scooted over as he lay down beside her and pulled the covers, which had been tossed aside at the slight sound she or her phone had made, over them both.

"Come here," he ordered when he saw her putting space between them. He opened up his arms and pulled her to his side. He tugged one of her arms over his bare stomach and held it there while he wrapped his other arm around her shoulders, and urged her to use his chest for a pillow. "You don't have to tell me to hold you. This is where I want you to be."

Reese burrowed into his heat. "This is where I want to be, too."

"I don't know what you see in me. But I'll be damned if I'm going to give you up without a fight."

He dropped a kiss to the crown of her hair, and

she turned her lips to kiss the swell of his pectoral muscle. "Whoever made you believe you aren't something special is wrong. I'm falling in love with you, Jackson Dobbs."

He grunted. Of course, he grunted.

Although she hadn't expected a confession in return, she was more worried that he was dismissing the legitimacy of her feelings for him. Stretching up, she cupped the side of his jaw and tilted his face toward hers. Then she closed the short distance between them and pressed a chaste kiss against his lips. When she pulled away, his lips chased hers and he planted a firmer stamp of possession on her mouth.

Then he threaded his fingers into her hair and guided her head back to the pillow of his chest. "Sleep, Freckles," he whispered. "He doesn't get to you tonight."

WHERE WAS SHE?

The man sat in the darkness outside Red's building and wondered why the lights hadn't gone on in her apartment. He rubbed his thumb up and down the etched steel blade of the knife he carried. He loved the feel of cold, hard metal almost as much as he loved the feel of a woman's soft body writhing beneath his. Even if she was as scared as he'd intended, running away from him, she should have been home by now.

He'd been nice to her today. She was almost ready to accept his next overture. She'd turn to him once she realized he was the only one who could protect her, the only one who could make her happy. She'd flashed those smiles and flirted with him for a reason. She wanted him.

He'd been with her tonight. He could have caught her in the light booth if he wanted. He could have chased her down and grabbed her before she ever made it to the back door. But she wasn't ready yet. He was still training her, bending her to his will, breaking her spirit if he had to. She had to learn how to be meek and compliant before she could be his.

All these years, he'd counted on one woman to keep his secret safe. It was fate that the knife had fallen into Red's hands. Now he was putting his fate in her hands. He wouldn't let her disappoint him.

He pulled out his phone and dialed her number. He watched the windows to see if a light came on. He waited with anticipation for her to answer.

He needed to hear her fear. He needed to hear what she would sound like when he made her his.

She had fight in her. She wouldn't surrender easily. But she would surrender.

Just like the others.

He'd tried to forge a relationship with Melora Dobbs. She'd wanted him. He could tell. But her husband stood in the way of them being together. He didn't realize Melora was still at the theater when he'd killed her husband. He had no idea she would try to protect him. No idea that she'd jump between him and his target and get stabbed herself. He'd held her while she bled, apologized, professed his love until he heard others coming and had to leave. The whore had lied to him. Led him on. Let him think they had a future together.

She'd spat in his face. Said she pitied him. Swore retribution in another life.

With her last breaths, she crawled to her dead husband and reached for his hand.

He'd been forced to turn to the one woman who would never betray him for help. He'd lived a good life, a successful life since then. But then the knife showed up in Reese Atkinson's theater.

He thought the woman he'd trusted had gotten rid of it twenty-three years ago. But she'd merely hidden it away. Had her conscience on her deathbed made her send the knife back to the theater to be found? Did someone else know his secret and plant the knife because they thought it was time for him to pay for his sins? Or was it truly just a freak accident that the expensive knife he'd sacrificed to get away with murder had been found and turned over to the crime lab by that righteous, troublesome redhead?

Finally, she picked up. "Hello?" He heard her breath catch. She tried to sound so brave, but she was crying. "I don't understand what you want. Why are you doing this to me?"

He stroked his knife blade as he listened to her breaking.

Then he heard a man's voice. "Hang up."

Startled, he cut the pad of his thumb on the blade's

edge. "No!" he muttered. The damn Dobbs man was interfering again!

The line went dead, and the rage built inside him, and his own blood dripped to the carpet at his feet.

Chapter Eleven

The next morning, Reese sat in the memorial lounge of the Kansas City Crime Lab, sipping her coffee while she watched the organized bustle of criminalists, scientists and police officers come and go to refill their mugs from a seemingly endless pot of coffee, grab a snack or sit down for a fifteen-minute tête-à-tête between meetings and experiments. Jackson had offered to let her sit in his office while he worked in the lab, but she preferred the sun streaming in through the windows and being around people.

She'd already made friends with an amazing dog named Blue, and gotten better acquainted with his KCPD handler, Aiden Murphy. This was the Murph Jackson had called when her car had been vandalized. She'd learned he was married to Jackson's team leader, Lexi Callahan-Murphy, and that he was the police officer assigned to safeguard crime scenes and the criminalists who worked them.

She also shared a conversation with Grayson Malone. The blood expert was a veteran Marine who walked with two prosthetic legs with crutches. He was more serious than Aiden had been, and had even grilled her with a few questions about how she and Jackson had met—she told him about the boy who'd loaned her a book, and the man who'd taken a murder weapon off her hands—and warned her that still waters run deep. But he skimmed over the fact that growing up in his uncle's house after losing his parents hadn't been a good experience for Jackson. When Reese pushed for more information, he told her to ask Jackson. Reese promised to do so and then asked Grayson if he was seeing anyone. He was proud to say that he was engaged to a fellow veteran who'd also dealt with a stalker, and that Allie Tate was the best thing that had ever happened to him. He stressed the importance of keeping Jackson in the loop on any strange feelings of being watched or threatening messages she received. That it was the lines of communication between him and Allie that had ultimately allowed him to rescue her when she'd been taken. Reese promised. And he laughed when she said she was learning to interpret Jackson-speak.

Chelsea O'Brien also stopped in to introduce herself. Reese had heard a lot of good things about the brilliant, talented computer geek. And while Reese knew she was an extrovert who got along well with most people, nothing could have prepared her for the gabfest that was Chelsea. She learned more about the lab; Jackson; Chelsea's fiancé, Buck, and their upcoming marriage; her dogs, who were named after Teenage Mutant Ninja Turtles; and two cats, Peanut Butter and Jelly, in fifteen minutes than she could learn in an entire semester of taking a class. The delightful woman wore glasses with colorful autumn leaves printed on them and an engagement ring that, while simple in design, had a good-sized diamond on it. She pulled up her laptop and showed Reese the tuxedo she'd ordered for Jackson for the party Saturday night and asked her to send a picture of him dressed in something besides jeans and a lab coat. Then Chelsea opened another screen with what looked like two sound wave patterns. Reese leaned in to pay close attention once she realized Chelsea was showing her information about *her* case.

"You were right," Chelsea said. "There were two different voices on the recording Jackson brought me from the theater. I peeled away the mechanical overtones and broke down the speech patterns. Based on pitch, one is male and one is female. Do you recognize either of these voices?"

Closing her eyes to focus on the faint, slightly slowed, voices, and not cringe at the threats she was hearing, Reese nodded. "The first voice is Dean Diamant. I was there when he recorded that for our show. He has such a distinctive voice." When it wasn't lecturing her or undermining her authority with her classes. The second voice made her a little sick to her stomach. "Could you play that one again?"

"Sure."

She heard Jackson's voice from the doorway. "It's Maisey Sparks, isn't it?"

She popped her eyes open and watched him stride toward her, his hand outstretched to take hold of hers.

"I believe so. But she can't be behind this terror campaign, can she? I don't think I'm worth that much time and effort in her eyes."

"She could have made the recording for someone else," Chelsea suggested. "For a friend or a professor. If she's the spoiled diva you describe, then maybe she did it for a lark."

Reese nodded. "I can see her doing that. Hell, I can see her doing that in exchange for getting a better grade in someone's class or to get another student to write a paper for her."

Jackson's steady strength seemed to seep right into her bloodstream from where their fingers touched. "Did you identify where the recording was made? Where the flash drive came from?"

"Somewhere on campus." Chelsea pushed her glasses onto the bridge of her nose. "I'm still working on narrowing it down to a specific computer. But I can tell you the rest of the flash drive contains files that have all been deleted."

"What kind of files?" Reese asked.

Chelsea hesitated.

But Jackson didn't. "What was in the files? I know you can retrieve lost data."

"Pictures. Lots and lots of pictures." Chelsea looked from Jackson down to Reese, her face wreathed with an apology. "Of you. Mostly at the theater. But some at your apartment building and running errands, I guess. It's not like you posed for any of them."

The temperature in the room dropped and Reese felt Jackson's arm slide around her shoulders. She reached over to fist her hand in the front of his lab coat. "How long has this been going on?"

"Is that a rhetorical question, or are you asking me?" Chelsea said.

"We're asking," Jackson stated.

Reese nodded.

"The first file was dated this summer. June."

"That's when I took over as theater manager. I'd finished all my PhD classes and the first draft of my dissertation. I've been at the theater almost every day since then."

"If it means anything," Chelsea added, "the pictures were all deleted yesterday afternoon. About the same time the second recording was added to the flash drive."

Reese loosened her grip on Jackson and reached over to squeeze Chelsea's hand. "Thank you."

The other woman blushed. "I'm just doing my job." She tilted her gaze to Jackson. "And helping out a friend."

Jackson nodded his thanks. "I want to know the minute you figure out which computer that recording came from."

"You will." Chelsea closed her laptop and hugged it to her chest. As she backed out the door, she pointed to Reese. "Make sure Jackson brings you to the wedding. You're officially invited."

"Thanks." Chelsea turned down the hallway and hurried to catch up with a man in a suit and tie. When the older man dipped his head to kiss her, Reese smiled. "I take it that's the fiancé?"

When Jackson didn't answer, she looked up to find him frowning down at her.

"What? What's wrong?" she prodded.

"Do I stay here and hold you? Or should I go back to work?"

Reese smiled at his dilemma. "I'm okay, Jackson. Just because I have the day off doesn't mean you don't have to work. I'm safe here, right?"

Jackson nodded. "You should be."

"Trust me, I can project a really loud scream if I do get in trouble."

"I'll hear you," he promised, either unaware or uncaring that she was teasing.

She leaned away to pull his arm from around her shoulders but kept hold of his hand. "Are you working on an important case?"

"I'm running the prints I took off the top of the light booth last night. And I want to compare the timeline of the threats you've received to the ones my mother did."

"Then you must go back to the lab. I'll be fine here." She glanced around. "I can make a fresh pot of coffee for everyone, and I've got some phone calls to make for the party tomorrow night."

"There are plenty of people around that theater who were there in one form or another twenty-three years ago."

"And there'll be even more tomorrow night." When it looked like he might say something about staying clear of the threat and not going, Reese reached up and touched the side of his face. "You'll be with me. I'll be safe."

He gave her the same curt nod he'd offered Chelsea.

Uh-uh. Their relationship was something more than friendship. She tapped his lips with her index finger, then brought it down to touch her own.

"You want me to kiss you in public?"

"Chelsea and Buck just did it," she reminded him. "I want you to kiss me anytime you want. And I fully intend on kissing you back."

"You're not embarrassed to be seen with me?"

She seethed as she imagined some witch in his past telling him that. No person who really knew Jackson could be embarrassed by his shy, gruff charm. That faceless female hadn't been kissed by him. Hadn't given him the chance to cherish her the way he did Reese. She wondered what it would take to make him see himself the way she did. Possibly just speaking as plainly and succinctly as he did, and showing him by her actions how important he was to her. "To be seen with a stud like you? Hell no. Now, are you going to kiss me, or what?"

The corner of his mouth crooked up in what she supposed passed for a smile. Then he released her grip and put one hand on the high tabletop and one hand on the back of the stool where she was sitting and leaned over her. "Oh, I'm kissing you, all right."

His lips covered hers with the same kind of driving heat he'd shown her last night. Reese brought her hands to his shoulders to hold on at the rush of sensations overtaking her. The kiss was brief. But it was hot. It was thorough. And Reese felt a little unsteady as he pulled away, his eyes hooded and locked on hers.

"Definitely a natural talent." She managed to find words as he licked his lips, as if he could taste her the way she could still taste him. She pushed him out of her space and swatted his backside. "Now get to work. I'll be waiting for you here when you're done."

She watched Jackson stride from the room back to his lab and knew she was in trouble. And not just from a stalker or a killer who might be trying to re-create history.

After forcing herself to get up and make the fresh pot of coffee she'd promised, Reese pulled up a familiar number on her phone and called her sister.

Regina "Reggie" Harrison was a married mother of two at home on maternity leave with her one-month-old baby. Reese got the scoop on the baby and two-year-old her sister was dealing with. Reggie sounded exhausted, but happy as she went on to tell Reese about how supportive her husband was, even though he'd had to go back to work full-time at the sheriff's office a couple of weeks ago.

Reese could tell by the decibels of noise dropping in the background that the baby had just gone down for a nap.

"All right." Reggie heaved a sigh and Reese hoped she had plopped down into a comfy chair. "We've got about twenty minutes before Ryne's video is done, so talk to me. I love you, but I also know you. And I can tell by the tone of your voice that there's something on your mind you want your big sister's opinion on. Please tell me it's a guy." When Reese didn't immediately answer, she imagined her sister sitting straight up. "Shut up. Tell me about him. Is he good to you?"

"Yes." Reese felt herself grow hot as she talked about Jackson. "He listens to me and talks to me like I'm an adult, and not a thirty-three-year-old version of a child star. He's quiet, but when he does say something, it has meaning. And can I tell you about the way this man is built?"

"Please. Lucas and I can't be together for another two weeks. I need something to distract me."

Reese laughed. Reggie and her husband had the kind of marriage Reese aspired to, one full of love and lust, unending support and mutual respect. She knew her sister would never look at another man, and Lucas would never stray to another woman.

"He's a little damaged by life. Some might say he looks like one of the mean, scarred-up henchmen in an action movie. He's tall and muscled. I mean, a lot of muscle—he used to be a heavyweight boxer in the Army. He had a traumatic childhood, and I think that's made him shy, reticent to reveal too much of himself. But he's not that way with me."

"He trusts you."

"I hope so. But it's all happening really fast."

"What's happening really fast? Sex? Pushing you for a commitment?"

"Me falling in love with him."

There was a long pause on the line, and then her sister said, "Tell me everything."

Reese did. She talked about the quiet boy who'd loaned her a book and encouraged her love of reading to their reunion at the crime lab. And though she shared a little bit about finding the knife and continuing to be on the butt end of some mean pranks, Reese focused on the part she needed to share with her sister. "Kissing him is like a meteor hitting the earth, and the world falls out from under your feet. Yet he's there to catch you."

"Good grief, Ree, now I'm feeling hot." Reggie took a long drink from her omnipresent water bottle before speaking again. "I think *I* love this guy."

"You've never even met him."

"I love him because he listens to you. He makes you feel good about yourself. And truly, Ree, this is the first guy since—what, we were teenagers?—who you've called and been this excited to tell me about." Before Reese could explain her concerns about getting closer to Jackson, Reggie issued an invitation. "When do I get to meet him? It doesn't take that long to drive halfway across the state and bring him to dinner here in Grangeport."

"I don't think I can get away right now. With work and the play—"

"Oh, we are totally coming to KC to see your play. He'll be there, right?" Reese hoped. "Have you asked him to come?"

"I'm hoping he will."

"Didn't I raise you better than that? You don't have to wait for a man to make the first move. Especially if he's shy like this one is. Oh, wait. Does he not like theater? That would be a deal breaker for you, wouldn't it?"

"I don't think he dislikes theater. I think he's not too fond of this one."

Reese could imagine the frown on Reggie's face. "He doesn't like the university?"

"You remember that college professor and his wife who were killed here?"

"Professor and Mrs. Dobbs? Yeah. Mom and Dad knew them. You did a show with him."

"They were Jackson's parents."

"Oh, sweetie." Her sister's enthusiasm ebbed, and concern took its place. "I remember going to the funeral. Mom stayed in New York with you, and Dad and I went to represent the family. I think half of Kansas City was there. Certainly, every professor and staff member from the university. He had an uncle there with him. But he still looked stoic. Alone. I don't think his extended family was much of a comfort to him."

"I don't think they were, either." In fact, they may have inflicted more damage on his vulnerable psyche when he'd needed their love and support. Her heart ached for the lonely boy he'd been. Since he hadn't mentioned his uncle, and Grayson Malone had suggested it wasn't a good relationship, she suspected they weren't close. Was it illogical to make the jump that once he'd lost his parents, Jackson hadn't had a good childhood? "I'm helping him reopen the case and find the killer."

"You're helping with a police investigation?"

"Crime lab investigation. They work together. But KCPD makes the arrest. Well, he's hoping with a couple of new leads, he can finally find out who murdered his mother and father."

"What about that other stuff you told me about last week? The weird gifts and messages."

"He's helping with that, too."

"I really like this guy. Listen to me, sweetie. You have to ask him out. Ask him to the show—or to help out with it, even. Fix him dinner and thank him for his efforts. You can't let him get away."

Reese chuckled at Reggie's adamant words. "That's your advice for your little sister? Knock Jackson over the head and drag him into my lair?"

"You said he's unsure of himself because of his looks—wait, he's not a total brute, is he?"

"No! He has beautiful, striking eyes."

"And you already mentioned all the muscles and the sexy voice." Reggie seemed to be evaluating everything Reese had told her. "He's protective of you and respectful?"

"Yes."

"Chase him until he catches you."

"Huh?"

"Just be yourself, sweetie. Let him see that big heart of yours. Give him the reassurance that he needs, then he'll turn the tables on you. He'll scoop you up in his arms and never let you go."

"What if he doesn't like me in that way?"

Reggie made a scoffing noise. "Are you kidding? You're my sister. You are talented and funny and smart, and your heart is bigger than you are. He'd be a fool to let you go. Besides, a man doesn't kiss a woman the way you described unless he likes her in *that way*."

"You don't think this is all happening too fast?"

"A piece of advice from your big sister?"

"Please."

"It doesn't matter how fast or slowly it happens. If he's the right guy, you grab on to him and hold tight."

Reese breathed out a sigh of relief. Her sister's words were reassuring since she was feeling the same way, too. This relationship with Jackson might be happening fast. But it also felt right. "Thanks, Reg. He's about to take his lunch break and drive me home so I can pack up some things for the next few nights. Thanks for the pep talk."

"Wait. You're staying at his place?"

"It's been just one night. I feel safer with him."

Reggie groaned. "You stayed the night with this guy, and you didn't lead with that?"

"All we did was sleep."

"Together?"

"Yes."

"Thanks for the juicy gossip. As much as I love my boys, I needed a break from changing diapers and answering all of Ryne's questions about the bugs he finds in the backyard. I love you, Ree."

"Love you, too, Reg. Hug my nephews and give my brother-in-law a kiss."

"I will. Now go get this guy." Reese was smiling from ear to ear as her sister hung up.

Jackson returned to the lounge, his white lab coat now replaced by his familiar leather jacket. "Ready?"

Reese drank him in for a moment, taking her sister's words to heart. *It doesn't matter how fast or slowly it happens. If he's the right guy, you grab on to him and hold tight.* She climbed down off her stool and hurried across the room to wind her arms around Jackson's waist and rest her cheek against his chest.

She was pleased to feel his arms settle lightly around her. "What's that for?"

"I just wanted to hug you. Claim you as mine, in case anyone is watching."

Misinterpreting her display of love as a reaction to some kind of threat, he tightened his hold and brushed his lips against the top of her hair. "The lab has security cameras inside and out. And the seventh precinct offices are connected to the other side of the complex. If that guy is anywhere around here, we'll catch him on surveillance. We'll get this guy."

Reese sighed against him, not wanting to correct him after such a fiercely protective tirade. "I know you will." Pulling back, she tilted her face to his. "But that's your serious look. You found out something?"

"I always have a serious look."

"Jackson." She tugged on the front of his jacket, demanding an answer. "What did you find out?"

"The fingerprints have no match in IAFIS."

"In what?"

"The Integrated Automated Fingerprint Identification System. So, we know our guy doesn't have a criminal record."

"You mean he hasn't been caught for anything."

He nodded. "There are other databases Chelsea is searching."

"Like university staff records. We were finger-printed and had background checks run on us when we were hired there."

He seemed hesitant to add the next bit of information. "My mother started receiving her anonymous love letters and threats about five months before she died."

Even with Jackson holding her, she felt the warmth inside her draining away. "You mean this is going to go on for another four and a half months?"

"Connecting whoever is after you to my parents' murders probably accelerated this guy's timeline."

"So, he could kill me sooner?" She was definitely feeling a chill now. "That's not reassuring."

He rubbed his hands up and down her arms. "Let my team do their thing. Let's go back to your apartment so you can pack a bag. I also need to pick up my tux for tomorrow."

"Jackson?" She didn't finish the question that weighed heavily on her mind until Jackson brushed the curls off her forehead and encouraged her to ask it. "What if we don't figure out who this guy is until it's too late?"

"I will be with you as much as I can. I notified the cold case squad that we were stirring up interest in my parents' murders, and they're sending a couple of detectives to work security at the reception tomorrow night. They'll be checking out suspects while they're there. And if I'm not with you, and he gets to you,

you fight. Just like you fought that creep who terror-
ized you as a child. Be relentless. Fight hard. Fight
dirty. And know that if you are not in my sight, and
I can't get a hold of you, I will be coming for you."

"What if he tries to hurt you? If he tries to get you
out of the way so that he can get to me? The way he
took out your father so he could get to your mom. If
it's the same guy."

Jackson stood there, a tall, overbuilt pillar of
strength who looked like he'd been bred for one thing.
Nodding, Reese reached up and touched the face she
loved. "You fight hard, too."

"I promise."

Chapter Twelve

Jackson Dobbs in a tuxedo was the kind of hot that made women pant with desire and men clear a path out of respect. Reese wished there was no party, no alumni or dean she had to cater to. She wanted nothing more than to take Jackson home and rip him out of that tux.

But that would be impractical. And bad for her job-performance review. And it might possibly put an end to her dream of finally earning her PhD.

No, tonight was the theater's big night, and she was in charge of making sure everything ran smoothly. Her student volunteers had all shown up on time, wearing costumes representing the series of plays for the season, or in suits or dresses if they worked backstage. The caterers had all the food she'd ordered to suit every taste and meet every dietary need of their guests. Champagne and sparkling grape juice were flowing, and the guests seemed to enjoy meeting old friends, getting to know the students and touring the theater.

Her own navy-blue gown had a modest neckline

that revealed a hint of cleavage, and a simple A-line design that flattered her full figure and was adorned with enough tiny glass beads that the thing felt like it weighed as much as her infant nephew. She carried her flute of sparkling grape juice through the crowd and inched her way toward Jackson, who stood at the wall at the back of the theater, where he could see her both through the open lobby doors to the food tables and displays there, and in the auditorium. The one time she'd led a group up to the light booth, Jackson had joined the tour.

There was something both wildly arousing and super comforting about having such intense focus directed on her throughout the evening. As long as she knew where that attention was coming from.

She sidled up beside him and leaned back against the wall. "Have you talked to anyone this evening? Or are you the tower of doom and gloom off in the corner?"

He dropped his hand down between them and closed it around her fingers. "I've run into some friends of Mom's and Dad's. They expressed their condolences, asked what I've been up to all these years."

Reese squeezed his hand. "I'm sorry. Is that hard for you?"

"I don't mind. The grief gave way to anger and determination a long time ago."

She leaned her head against his shoulder. "I was worried about the crowd being too much for you. I didn't think about the bad memories."

"I'm making good memories now." His gaze

continually scanned their surroundings, though he paused to exchange a nod with Max Krolikowski, one of the detectives from the cold case squad here tonight. "Once people discover I'm with you tonight, they rave about what a fantastic job you've done here, and how proud of you I must be." He tilted his head to press a soft kiss to the crown of her hair. "I am."

"Thank you. I wonder if any of the powers that be will notice."

"There are bigger players here than Dean Diamant," he pointed out. "You have the ability to work the room and make everyone from a lowly freshman to your most generous donor feel welcome and important. People notice."

Two of those people she'd worked hard to impress chose that moment to approach her. Reese released Jackson's hand and smiled at the two gentlemen who'd traveled all the way from the theater district in New York to be here tonight. "Mr. McKay. Mr. Haight. I trust you're enjoying your evening?"

"We're having a great time," George Haight, the taller one with the graying hair answered. "The dean may have gotten a little long-winded for my tastes, and Simon was understandably teary-eyed by the unveiling of the theater's new name, but otherwise, it's been a perfectly fine reception."

The shorter, pudgier man with the receding hairline, Linus McKay, echoed the praise. "I've enjoyed talking directly to the students. I'm sure some of them know I'm an agent and are trying to impress me, but for the most part I'm simply reassured to see such a love and knowledge of the theater being instilled in them."

"We do our best." They practically ignored Jackson, but since he didn't seem to mind looked unbothered, she didn't make a big deal out of it. "We're honored that you'll be here this week to sit in on rehearsals and be a guest speaker in some of our classes."

"Yes, yes." Linus snapped his fingers a couple of times, as if he was trying to recall something. "Do you mind if we ask you a question?"

She felt Jackson's hand slide against the small of her back, shielding her, she supposed, if the question proved upsetting. "If I can answer, sure."

George Haight jumped into the conversation. "I've seen you on Broadway, haven't I?"

"Ages ago."

Linus seemed pleased that she'd confirmed their suspicions. "You starred in the revival of *Annie*, and then did a turn in a drama. What was it?"

"*The Innocents*."

"Critics loved you. You could have had a long career." A comment once made by her own agent at the time. "Why did you leave?"

She drifted back against the warmth of Jackson's hand. "It was a personal choice. My parents died tragically. I was only fourteen. I needed to be home with my family."

"That's rough. I'm so sorry to hear that." Mr. McKay's sympathy sounded genuine. "Hey, but making it in academia is no small potatoes, either. And now you're inspiring the next generation. That's an awesome calling."

Mr. Haight finally turned the conversation to a less personal topic. "My company sponsors a grant to support theater programs in academic settings. Have you ever considered applying?"

"Really? We're always looking for funding..."

The conversation tapered away, when Reese felt a pair of eyes boring into her like bullets seeking their target. She turned her head to see Maisey Sparks at the end of the aisle.

And she was pissed that Reese was getting the attention of the New York producer and agent.

AFTER MAISEY HAD run off after her uncle Dix to no doubt complain about Reese stealing her opportunity to go to New York, Reese concluded the conversation with the two men. She excused herself from Jackson as well to continue mingling with other guests.

But a peaceful end to her evening was apparently too much to ask for. Once she handed a check over to the lead caterer and told them it was okay to start clearing away their things except for the coffee and desserts that some guests were still enjoying, she made her way back into the theater to the spot where she last saw Jackson chatting with the two detectives.

Instead of finding the three men talking police business, she saw Maisey Sparks wagging her finger at Jackson and spewing lies that would have diminished a lesser man. And bless his heart, Jackson just stood there frowning, as if he wasn't sure what recourse he had against a girl nearly half his age having a temper tantrum. It would be ungentlemanly to simply walk away. And arguing back wasn't really his thing.

A protective rage reenergized her body. She was exhausted, her heels had been pinching her toes for about an hour too long and she was livid to hear the twenty-year-old going after Jackson when she'd been unable to get her satisfaction with her.

"You know Ms. A is only with you because she needs a bodyguard."

Reese did the thing she'd seen Jackson do many times when he was protecting her. She put herself between Jackson and the threat that was getting on her last nerve. She had no trouble tilting her chin and letting Maisey have it. "You are a spoiled, immature brat who doesn't know thing one about what a real man is like. You don't speak to my man with respect? Then you don't speak to him at all."

"Your man? You must be good in bed, Beast," the young woman sneered.

Reese didn't bat an eye. She simply leaned closer and articulated two words. "He is."

Not that she knew that for a fact, but she suspected he would be, given the way he kissed and held her. Besides, she hadn't been lying when she'd told the student to button her lip unless she could speak to Jackson with respect.

Maisey sputtered through the beginning of one sentence, and then another, before she shook her long hair down her back and retreated a step. "My grandfather wants to speak to you."

"Oh?"

"He's up onstage."

"Maybe you should go to New York, Maisey, and forget about college theater." Reese could ignore her role as a mentor and teacher completely. "Just know that it's a lot scarier out there in the big world when you're trying to make a living doing this. No matter how much you love it. No matter how much you want to succeed. No matter how hard you try. There will be a hundred other girls, just as talented, just as pretty, fighting just as hard as you for the same part. And no one in New York will be as supportive of you, or will try to teach you as much as I have."

Maisey literally growled before she gestured up to the stage and stormed away. "Just go."

Reese didn't take a deep breath until the young woman was out of earshot and she felt Jackson's big hands on either side of her waist.

"Her words didn't bother me, Freckles, because her opinion doesn't matter to me. I know she's got issues and is lashing out." She felt Jackson's warm breath tickle her ear and she shivered. "But do you know how hot it is to hear you leap to my defense like that?"

Reese didn't turn to face him. They still had guests, and jumping his bones right now shouldn't be part of the show they'd come to see. "You think I'm hot?"

His teeth closed gently around her earlobe next to the sapphire earring she wore. She gasped and goose bumps erupted up and down her arms. "I don't know if I'm good or not. I've never gotten an official evaluation. But with the right teacher, I'd be willing to try."

With that offer, Reese did turn around. "Are you serious?"

Jackson grunted. That was a yes.

Reese beamed him a smile. "I have no doubt you will ace the class."

Jackson leaned over to kiss the top of her head. "Go. Meet with Mr. Lowry. I'll be here when you're ready to go home."

"Did the detectives find out anything new?"

He shooed her away. "Ticktock, Professor. Only another half hour and I can take off this damn bow tie and find out how many freckles are underneath your dress."

Reluctantly, Reese headed down the aisle to the stage one more time. By this time of night, her middle toes were numb and the small of her back ached from being on her feet for so many hours today. Still, with Jackson watching over her and the promise of making love somewhere in her future, she felt energized by the time she stepped up onto the stage and approached the white-haired gentleman who was admiring the Beatrice Lowry Theater sign.

She smiled as Simon Lowry turned to her. "Maisey said you wanted to see me?"

Simon reached for her hands and held both of them in his gnarled fingers. "Yes. I wanted to have a private conversation with you."

Reese glanced around the set where they were standing. "In the middle of the stage?"

Although he chuckled at her incredulity, he quickly dropped his voice to a soft tone she could barely hear and got serious. "I know this seems exposed, but Dix assured me the microphones were all turned off so that no one can hear us. And no one will be suspicious as they would be if we wander off to someplace on our own."

As she leaned closer to hear him, one word popped out. "Suspicious?"

Although he didn't turn his face from hers, his eyes were looking in every direction. The older man *was* afraid of being overheard. "Watch your back, Professor Atkinson. I thought I was doing the right thing. My wife had hidden that knife for all these years. I've always known. But I would never betray my Beatrice. I would never give away what she had done. She was protecting someone she loved."

"What are you talking about, Mr. Lowry?" Reese was confused. What did this wealthy old widower know about the knife she'd found?

"I put it in the box and sent it to the theater for someone to find. When Beatrice died, I thought justice could finally be served. Secrets could be revealed. But I fear all I've done is turn you into a target."

Reese stepped closer. Was this the witness Jackson had been waiting for to step forward? "Mr. Lowry. Who killed Everett and Melora Dobbs? Who was your wife hiding the knife for?" A shadow swung over them and back again. It wasn't unusual for shadows to be created when the stage lights were on. But that unusual shape wasn't similar to any prop or set piece in her play. When the shadow darkened Simon Lowry's head again, she looked up into the fly space and saw the danger swinging over them. "Move!"

She shoved the old man aside as Zach Oliver's beautiful gargoyle came crashing down. The weight of several two-by-fours clipped Reese's right shoulder and she fell on top of Simon. She curled into a ball as everything from her elbow down to her fingers went instantly numb. The frayed rope that had held the gargoyle so precariously in place tumbled down after, and she ducked her head again. Simon howled with agony as the gargoyle lost its head and splintered into a dozen pieces.

"Reese!" She heard Jackson's shout.

Zach ran up onto the stage and knelt beside his masterpiece. "My gargoyle."

"Don't touch that!" Jackson warned, racing down to the stage. "It's evidence. Back away, son."

"Yes, sir." Zach hovered over Reese, muttering apology after apology. "Ms. A, I'm so sorry. I didn't do that. I swear. I'm so sorry."

"It's all right, Zach. I believe you." She reached up to squeeze Zach's hand and reassure him, and slowly pulled herself up to a sitting position. "You go down and sit in one of the seats. I'll ask the police if we can salvage it."

The numbness in her shoulder turned into a sharp, shooting pain as feeling returned. The tips of her fingers tingled, and even the small of her back protested the sudden pain radiating outward from where she'd been struck. She looked over to see Simon rolling back and forth on the floor, cradling his arm against his stomach. Although his son, Dix, was kneeling beside him, Reese pushed herself up onto her hands and knees and crawled toward him. "Mr. Lowry? Mr. Lowry, are you hurt?"

Before she could reach him, a rough hand grabbed her around the upper arm and hauled her to her feet. Reese cried out in pain as Dean Diamant shouted angry words at her. "What the hell were you thinking? You broke the man's wrist."

"I saved his life," she argued, trying to twist away from his painful grasp. "I'm fine, too, thanks for asking."

"Don't you get smart with me." He wrenched her arm, aggravating her injury, and she cried out. "He means millions to us."

"Ow! Let go of me!"

"You don't touch her!"

A meaty fist flew past Reese's face and plowed into Dr. Diamant's jaw, freeing her from his harsh grip and knocking him to the floor.

Then Jackson was carefully pulling her around the wreck of Zach's prop. "Are you hurt? Where did it hit you?"

"My shoulder. I'll be fine. Maybe an ice pack and an ibuprofen later. Check on Mr. Lowry."

"Lowry's not my responsibility."

She clutched at the lapel of Jackson's tuxedo jacket and tugged him closer so she could whisper. "He said he's the one who sent the knife to the theater for me to find. That his wife had been hiding it for somebody all this time."

His eyes narrowed with a question.

Reese shook her head. "He didn't say who she was covering for. That's when the gargoyle dropped. Like someone knew what he was saying to me and wanted to shut him up."

"Or maybe Dix was looking to get his inheritance early."

"Will he be okay? We can still ask questions."

"His son is looking after him, and the EMTs are on their way." Jackson glanced over at the remains of the gargoyle Zach was stewing over, then up into the ceiling above them. "I need to get a look at that rope and find out how somebody got that up there."

"There's a tall ladder in the back. But that shouldn't be there. It's not part of the show, and the prop we do drop is a lot lighter and hangs upstage beyond the garden doors." She scoured the crowd, looking for an angry young woman. "Maisey was pretty pissed at me."

"She wouldn't have been able to hang that up there without us seeing her."

"It had to be hung before the reception started."

"You have a list of everyone who was scheduled to speak onstage?"

She nodded. "Simon and Dixon Lowry. Dean Diamant. The president of the university."

"You."

"Patrick."

Scowling, Jackson surveyed the crowd again.

"Where is your wannabe boyfriend? I haven't seen him around for a while."

Reese tugged on his lapel. "He's not my boyfriend. You are."

He covered her hand with his. "I know that. But does Brown?"

Reese took in the chaos around the stage—Zach bemoaning the destruction of his artwork, Dixon Lowry keeping anyone from getting too close to his father, who was lying on the stage, and everyone circling around to get a better look or express their concern. Dr. Diamant sat in one of the chairs that were part of the set, cradling his bruised jaw and rubbing at something in his pocket, probably a stress ball that wasn't doing him a damn bit of good, all the while glaring at her.

"Jackson? I want to go home. Your home. I want to get out of here."

"We can't just yet, hon. You'll need to give a statement to the police."

With her strength quickly ebbing and fear and suspicion seeping in to take its place, Reese leaned heavily against Jackson's arm. Had someone just tried to kill her? Or Simon Lowry? Or was this accident yet another fluke occurrence that happened around her at the theater?

It didn't feel like an accident. And it didn't feel like anyone else had to worry about someone wanting to kill them.

"Now, Jackson. I can't do this anymore."

She felt his eyes studying her. And then he peeled

off his jacket, draped it over her shoulders and pulled it together beneath her chin. "Okay. I'll tell the detectives that we're leaving, and call someone else from the lab in to process this mess. Will you be okay to hang out here while I bring my truck around?"

She nodded, but Jackson didn't look convinced.

"Zach, is it?" he asked of the young man sitting a few rows back in the auditorium.

"Yes, sir?"

Jackson helped her down the steps and into the seat next to Zach's. "Will you sit with Professor Atkinson and hold her hand until I can come back in to get her? And don't let anyone bump into her right shoulder. It must be pretty bruised."

"Is she okay?"

"She will be." Jackson dropped his head to claim her lips in a quick, hard kiss before he jogged back onto the stage toward the back door. "If I have anything to say about it, she will be."

SOME TIME LATER, after a hot shower, a cold ice pack and a few hours of blessedly mindless sleep snugged in Jackson's arms, Reese awoke before dawn to the repetitive stroke of Jackson's fingers running up and down her arm.

Sometime during the night, the giant T-shirt she wore had slipped off her shoulder to expose the dark-gray-and-violet-red evidence of where the heavy gargoyle prop had slammed into her. She propped her chin on his chest and raised her gaze to his to show him that she knew he was upset. "Jackson? Are you all right?"

He grunted. "You're not. That bruise on your shoulder is the size of my fist. If that thing had hit you in the head…"

"But it didn't. I'm sorry if it upsets you, but the bruise will fade, and I'll be just fine."

His fingers traveled all the way up her arm, skipped her injury and settled beneath the fringe of her hair to cup the nape of her neck. "What can I do to make this better?"

"Keep your promise."

"What promise haven't I kept? You know my word is good."

"I know. But you've been worried about me, and I've been snoring on your shoulder, and you may have forgotten. Tonight, at the reception, you indicated that you wanted to make love to me." She might have started this conversation, but she was the one blushing with heat. "Well, actually, I think you said something about counting all the freckles underneath my dress."

His arms shifted around her to hug her more tightly against him. "I want that more than you know."

"Ask me, Jackson. Ask and I'll say yes. I want to forget everything for a while—the messages, the so-called accidents, solving a murder. I want to focus on the best part of these past few days. Finding you."

The long fingers at her nape played with her hair. "I love your hair. It's silky and soft. It curls around my fingers and clings to them. And that fiery color is all you, isn't it." She nodded, loving the words that came out of this taciturn man's mouth when he did choose to speak. "Reese Atkinson, I want to make love to you. Will you let me?"

"Let you? I'm about to beg you."

He shifted in the bed beside her, forcing her to rest her cheek rather than her chin against him. Maybe he didn't want to look her in the eye when he told her this. "My uncle Curtis used to tell me I wasn't special enough for any woman to want me."

"He's the man who raised you?" He nodded. She hugged her arm around his waist more tightly. "There's something wrong with him for saying that to a child. You believed him, though, didn't you?"

"It was either shine like a star or you didn't exist in Curtis Graham's house." He laughed, but there was no humor in his tone. "I was a homely kid. Too tall and skinny to be able to coordinate everything. I didn't love sports the way he did. Even after I started filling out, his opinion didn't change. I had no chance of earning his love."

"For the record? I hate your uncle Curtis."

"You do get fired up on my behalf, don't you?"

"Red hair," she teased, suspecting he could tell her temper wasn't the reason she felt so protective of him. "What did you do to get away from Uncle Curtis and his wrong way of thinking?"

"I joined the Army and started punching things."

Reese laughed. There was a wry sense of humor hiding inside this man. She propped herself up on her elbows, resting one beside him and one against his chest so she could look into those beautiful gray eyes again. "What did it feel like punching Dean Diamant? I've often wanted to do that. But I didn't think I was strong enough. Or I was worried I'd get fired."

He grinned. "After the way I've heard him talk to you, it felt pretty damn good."

"I imagine."

But the grin quickly faded. His fingers were stroking up and down her back now, tangling in her hair, then traveling down to rest against the curve of her rump. "When he put his hands on you and you cried out in pain, I'd had enough. I'm sorry if that gets you into trouble at the school."

"I wouldn't worry about it. His idea of mentoring a PhD student has strayed a long way from supporting and challenging the doctoral candidate. There is a whole new generation of harassment laws I can cite against him. He might even have defied the school's policies on plagiarism and underage drinking."

"You think you could get him fired?" His hand squeezed her bottom. She liked the weight of his hand there.

"He does have tenure, so it wouldn't be easy. But I don't want to talk about him anymore. I want to talk about us. And freckle exploration."

She rode the rise and fall of his chest as he took in a deep breath. "As willing as I am, I don't have a lot of experience with this," he admitted.

"Because of your uncle not understanding what a treasure you are?" She drew her fingers around the stubble of his jaw and decided he wasn't a beast, at all. He had an interesting face, marked by life and tragedy and what she hoped were a few good memories. It was the face she wanted to look at every morning when she woke up. "But you do have some experience?" He nodded, though his expression remained grim. "It wasn't good?"

"We both got off if that helps."

"You can get off without having an emotional attachment or feeling fulfilled."

"I was a notch in her bedpost. A bet with her friends. She was gone before I woke up in the morning. That's just one of my misadventures with the fairer sex."

Reese hugged him as tightly as she could in this awkward position. "I hate that woman, whoever she was. She's not related to Maisey Sparks or your uncle Curtis, is she? I bet you didn't kiss her the way you've kissed me. No woman in her right mind would leave you if you kissed her like that." Reese started to pull away when she heard the vehemence in her own voice. "But I don't want you practicing on anyone else."

His arms tightened around her, anchoring her in place. "I don't want to practice on anyone else, either."

Good they were on the same page when it came to attraction and fidelity. She smiled at that. "Would you like to see my freckles now?" He nodded and Reese pushed his arm away to sit up on her knees beside him. She tugged her shirt off and tossed it to the foot of the bed. Feeling suddenly self-conscious about baring herself to him, she crossed her arms in front of her to cover her breasts. He might not think himself handsome, but she had too many pounds on too small a figure she wished she could hide. "Sorry. I'm kind of bouncy and soft."

He pulled her hands away and sat up facing her. His eyes were glued to her breasts. "You're perfect." He cupped her breasts the way she just had. Only his touch had everything to do with praise and seduction, not modesty. "I've got big hands, and these fill them." He teased her nipples between his thumbs and the palms of his hands until they tightened into stiff peaks, and she moaned with pleasure that darted straight down to her womb. Then he drew a line into her cleavage and pushed her breasts aside. His observations sounded very scientific, but every caress was fueling the tension inside her. "You do have freckles everywhere." He brushed the underside of one breast, stroked his thumb across the nipple of the other, then buried his nose between her breasts and pressed his lips to one lucky spot. "Here. Here. And here."

"Jackson." She breathed his name as her pulse jumped into hyperdrive and her panties dampened with heat.

"I'm a big man. And you're so petite."

"You'll fit, Jackson. A woman's body is made to stretch and be filled by the person she's making love with. If she's properly prepared."

"With my hand or mouth?"

Just the words made her squirm with desire. She nodded. She wound her arms around his neck and pulled him down to the mattress on top of her. His muscular thigh settled at the juncture of her legs, putting delicious pressure on that most sensitive part of her.

He started to retreat, but she held on tighter. "You're better at this than you know, big guy. How about we start with a kiss."

He dipped his head and proceeded to make her mindless with desire. He trailed kisses down to her breasts. Her hands fisted in his hair and she cried out his name. "What about here?" He pressed a kiss to her stomach, then nudged aside the waistband of her sweats with his nose. "Found more."

He tugged her pants off her hips and one leg. He kissed the seam of her thigh and licked the crease there.

"Jackson!"

"You do have freckles from head to toe." Then he bent her leg at the knee and pushed it up toward her body, exposing her weeping center to his gaze. "Like this?"

"Like what?" Reese squealed a senseless moan as his mouth closed over her sensitive bud. After bringing her to orgasm that way, he shucked off his pants, rolled on a condom and settled himself where she most wanted him to be.

"You sure you're ready for me?"

Still riding the roller coaster that his hands and mouth had taken her on, she made a guttural sound in her throat.

He grinned above her. "A grunt is not an answer."

She grinned, too, wrapping her legs around his

hips and digging her heels into his backside. "Now, Jackson. I want *you* right now." He thrust himself inside her and proceeded to take her on another round of the roller coaster she would ride again and again. "I love you, Jackson," she whispered against his skin before she flew off the tracks and into arms she trusted would catch her and never let her go.

Chapter Thirteen

Dress rehearsal Thursday night had been full of miscues—an actress coming onstage in the wrong costume, an actor saying his act 3 monologue during act 2, a supposedly "dead" actor onstage having a sneezing fit and making it pretty near impossible for the other actors onstage—including Maisey—to keep a straight face and move on with the show. In other words, as theater lore would say, a bad dress rehearsal made for a great opening night.

"You guys are ready for this." Reese had taken no director's notes to share with her cast and crew. At this point, there was nothing for her to polish or improve. She needed to let them do their thing. "Thank you for all your hard work. You're going to knock the socks off our audiences this week and next. Hang up your costumes, put away your props, then go home and get a good night's sleep. I'll see you tomorrow for makeup call and sound checks starting at six. Remember, no alcohol, no milk. Drink lots of water. You need to protect your voices for the run of the show."

There was a general chorus of thank-yous and

good-nights before the cast and crew left the stage to change in the dressing rooms or reset the equipment for tomorrow night.

Once the last student had disappeared from sight, Reese stretched her arms out to the side and exhaled a weary sigh.

"Your job is done now, right?"

She turned to their lone audience member and smiled as Jackson came down the aisle to hug her tightly enough to lift her onto her toes before he claimed her mouth in a kiss.

There had been a lot of that this week. Hugging. Kissing. Making out when she was tired from the last long rehearsals before opening night when she integrated the tech aspects of the show, such as sound and lighting, into the production. They'd even made love a couple of times when she wasn't so exhausted. Every time she smiled at him, or she took his outstretched hand, she could see the curse of his childhood lifting from his shoulders layer by layer. If she was patient, if he could finally believe that her feelings for him were real, permanent—then Reese might just find her happily-ever-after. Since the launch-party reception, Jackson had come to the theater with her every night except for the one time he and his team had gotten called to work a crime scene outside a bar in a rough part of town. And that night, he'd asked his friend Aiden Murphy, and Aiden's K-9 partner, Blue, to sit in on rehearsal and drive her to Jackson's house when she was done.

"That's the idea," she answered, once her boots

touched the floor again. "I've prepared them as best I can. It's their show now."

Jackson followed her onto the stage and picked up a couple of the irreplaceable props and then stowed them in her office after she unlocked the door. The one thing marring her chance at happiness was a big thing—a lot bigger than the gargoyle that had come crashing down on her.

She still hadn't identified the man who was terrorizing her.

And they weren't any closer to finding the man who'd killed Jackson's parents.

The information Simon Lowry had given her had turned out to be a dead end because Dixon Lowry had hired a lawyer, and as long as his father was in the hospital recovering from the surgery on his broken wrist, he wasn't letting him talk to the police or the crime lab or anybody.

Could a relationship between them survive if they never found answers?

Jackson's coworker Chelsea had scoured the records of old newspapers and campus publications to search for any mention of a man tied to Beatrice Lowry besides her husband whom Beatrice would care enough about to help cover up a murder. There was her son, Dixon, of course. And numerous social gatherings and fundraisers that listed most of the people on their suspect list. Dean Diamant, Patrick Brown and Dix had been students or faculty at the university twenty-three years ago. As dear as she'd found Simon to be, he, too, had experience in the theater. What if he was just acting the part of a sweet old man, deflecting suspicion onto someone else after losing track of the murder weapon?

As for pricey knife collections? After the attack during the reception, a judge had issued four search warrants to go through Patrick Brown's tools and comb through Dean Diamant's home and office. Not that that had earned her any brownie points with her coworkers.

If anything, the pressure the KCPD and the crime lab were putting on the investigation was making her stalker more and more unhappy with her. She was getting the creepy phone calls every night now. She wanted to get a new phone number, but Jackson had insisted that the best way to track down this guy was to keep him focused on her. He took her phone the second they knew it was him and carried it into another room so she wouldn't have to listen. While the call was active, the lab could run a trace. They all led back to more disposable cell phones, but Chelsea could pinpoint that the calls were all pinging off the same two cell towers—either the one by her apartment building, or the one closest to the theater. He was definitely following her. Definitely watching for his chance to…what? Make good on any one of the threats he'd made?

"You've got that pensive, hopeless look on your face again." Jackson slipped his arms around her from behind and rested his chin on her shoulder. "We'll get this guy. I promise."

Reese leaned back into his strength for a few seconds before pushing him away. "Will you stay with me once you do?"

"What?"

"Never mind." She stuffed her bag into the bottom drawer of her desk and tucked her keys into her pocket. "I need to make the rounds. Make sure all the students have left and all the doors are locked."

But the doorway was blocked by Jackson's bulky, unyielding body. "Do you doubt my feelings for you?"

Reese drifted back a step and threw her hands out in exasperation. "One of these days you're going to figure out you're not a beast and you can have any beauty you want."

"I don't want anyone else. I wouldn't trust anyone else to accept me the way I am."

"Oh, well, then you're going to get tired of me. Tired of being with the woman who's always the victim. Tired of being with the woman who has to be watched over 24/7."

"Honey, you're exhausted, frustrated and scared."

"Yeah, I am. And, apparently, that's never going to change."

Jackson's eyes narrowed as he leaned toward her. "You've gone to the dark place where I usually reside. I don't like seeing you there."

"That's just too damn bad, Jackson Dobbs."

"Freckles—"

"Don't call me that stupid nickname!"

"Is there a problem here?" Patrick Brown walked up behind Jackson. He wore his tool belt and clasped a hammer in his fist as if he'd armed himself with a weapon.

Jackson turned, planting himself squarely between Reese and anyone he deemed a threat. If that hammer had been a screwdriver or a pocketknife... Reese almost felt like she was flashing back to a remembered attack. Only, she'd never been stabbed. But she'd seen something, hadn't she? Still, the answers wouldn't come, and whatever she thought was important about that memory blipped out of her head.

"No. There's no problem. Just a disagreement." She walked up to Jackson, linked her arm through his and nudged him aside so that she could leave her office. "Everything's fine, Patrick. You can head on home. I'll check the doors." She glanced up at Jackson. "Why don't you go ahead and get your truck and pull it up to the end of the sidewalk."

Jackson nodded, then grabbed his jacket and followed Patrick. "I'll walk out with you."

Reese felt a flare of annoyance as much as she felt relief that Jackson was making sure she was alone in the building while she made her rounds. Even after she'd picked that stupid fight with him, he was intent on keeping her safe. God, he was a good man. And he had no idea what a catch he was. She'd cleared and locked up both dressing rooms and the greenroom before she heard the back door close behind the two men. She hastened her steps. She needed to apologize to Jackson and explain her own insecurities that had popped up out of sheer frustration and fatigue before her hurtful words drove him back to that grunting, uncommunicative man she'd first met.

Moving with a purpose once again, Reese hurried to secure the lobby doors and run up to the light box she hated so much now, and make sure that door was locked, too.

She was striding across the stage to her office when she heard the sound of clapping coming from the back of the auditorium. One pair of hands. One man. Applauding her.

Feeling dread a hundred times worse than the night she'd heard the skewed nursery rhyme recorded for her, Reese turned.

Dean Diamant must have been hiding in his darkened office. She hadn't seen him, hadn't even known he was in the building tonight. He stopped clapping when she made eye contact with him, and found she couldn't look away.

"Dean," she greeted him, her tone light and surprisingly friendly despite her trepidation. "I didn't see you there." *Good acting job, Reese.* "Were you watching rehearsal? I think we've got a good show."

"You…are a thorn in my side, Ms. A. Reese— I'm never going to call you *Professor*—Atkinson. In my mind you'll always be Red, from the day you first waltzed into my office and batted your eyes at me to the day you die. You're my Red."

"Excuse me?" Reese turned her body slightly away from him and pulled her phone from her pocket. She slid it down her leg where she could call up a number without drawing attention to it. Jackson was the last person she'd texted so his name should be at the top of her call list. She tapped his number. Now what? She couldn't text without looking at her phone, and she couldn't call him without the ringing and his answering giving her away. "I've never batted my eyes at anybody in my life. And I'm not *your* anything." Her gaze dropped to the bandage on his thumb. He'd had that on the night of the reception. Had he cut himself? And what was he clutching so hard between his fingers and palm? He had a knife. That's what he'd been fiddling with the night of the reception, working out his fury on an object that was precious to him. He was carrying a knife.

She ended up texting the buttons she could reach without looking. Probably pure gibberish. She hit Send, typed in more random letters and hit Send again. The messages wouldn't make any sense. But maybe Jackson would be curious enough to come see why she was repeatedly butt-texting him.

Dean just kept walking, moving step by step down the aisle, coming closer. The bruise from Jackson's fist was still visible on his jaw, and the dark look in his eyes stripped away any hints of handsome there. Who was the Beast now?

"Don't bother calling him," he warned.

"Calling who?"

"Your boyfriend. That Neanderthal. The son of my worst enemy and the woman I loved more than my own life."

"Really? If you loved Melora more than your own life, how come she's dead and you're here?" Where was this snarky sarcasm coming from? *Don't poke the beast*, part of her brain warned. The other part urged her to get in his face and tell him she was done letting him ruin her life—letting him ruin Jackson's, as well.

"He can't get to you to you to help now. He can't lay me out flat with one of those brawny fists."

"Don't count on it."

He laughed, but there was far more evil than amusement in the sound. "You've locked him out, my dear. I asked Patrick to make sure he left because I thought he was bothering you. And now he can't get back in, even if he somehow knew you needed him. You've done such a fine job as theater manager that this place is locked up tight every night. Unless, of course, he has a key."

Okay. That was a problem. Jackson didn't have a key. Was Patrick still outside with him with his keys? She had the feeling that Jackson had been intent on making sure Patrick was off the premises while she was here. Could Jackson reach campus police in time to do an emergency breach of the doors to get to her before Dean Ego Pants did?

"You loved Melora Dobbs?"

"With all my heart. I killed Everett to get him out of the way. She wasn't supposed to be here that night. She had a little boy at home to take care of. She wasn't supposed to try to stop me. She wasn't supposed to get in the way."

"How could you let someone you love die like that?"

"Because I knew there'd be others. Instead of saving herself, instead of loving me, she spat in my face and crawled to her husband."

"Others?"

"It has been twenty-three years, Red. Do you honestly think a man like me can't have any woman he wants? Patrons. Other professors. Students. Most cooperated."

Most? What happened to the others, like her, who refused to fall at his feet? Swallowing the bile that threatened to choke her at Dean's selfish explanation for the end of two innocent lives, and possibly more, she asked, "Why did you give the knife to Beatrice Lowry?"

"Because we were lovers back then. She had a soft spot for me."

"I bet she had a bigger soft spot for this theater and keeping scandal away from the place she loved so much."

"You think you're so smart. But you never did see the truth, did you, Red?"

"Reese."

He ignored her and kept advancing. "I wanted to mentor you. I wanted to be your friend. I wanted to be lovers."

She was choking again. By the time she cleared her throat, she heard knocking at the back door. She almost glanced back. But Dean had heard the noise, too.

"Hmm. He's worried. He's suffering. Your big, strong man can't get to you now."

"He's not just strong. He's smart. He's resourceful."

"He's outside."

Right. Chilling thought. Bad guy with knife. She needed to do something here or she was going to wind up bleeding to death like Melora Dobbs. She wouldn't inflict that nightmare twice on any man, especially the man she loved.

"So, Beatrice Lowry was your first lover. Makes sense. You probably met at some theater event. Then she realized how much money she'd lose, or custody of her children, if Simon ever found out. So, she broke it off with you. Then you turned to Melora for comfort over getting dumped for a better man. But she wouldn't give you the time of day. With your ego, you couldn't imagine her not wanting you. There had to be another reason for her turning you away. It must be the husband. How am I doing so far?"

"Pretty accurate. But you'll never be able to prove anything."

"Your blood will match the unidentified blood on that knife."

"I won't give them my blood."

"Well, they're going to know you did a bad thing today," she challenged as he reached into his pocket and pulled out an unusually long ivory-handled pocketknife, and flipped it open.

"But they don't know I'm here. All those pranks you complained to me about, those clever messages—I was here all the time and you never even realized. The only one who knows the hidey-holes and hidden stairwells of this theater better than you is me." Reese tried to quell the panic rising in her veins. That knife looked very, very sharp. "No one knows I'm here tonight except you. When I'm done, no one will find me here. All they'll find is your dead body."

"You're going to kill me because I wouldn't date you?"

"No, Red. I'm going to kill you because you wouldn't cooperate. You wouldn't turn to me for help when those messages started coming. You wouldn't let me comfort you. All you gave me were problem students and you whined about the jobs I asked you to do. I'm going to kill you because you found that damn knife before I could and then you turned it over to the police."

"The crime lab."

Correct terminology didn't matter. "Once I knew that Simon had known about the knife and me all these years, I thought I could get rid of you both before he blabbed the truth to the world."

Reese heard the pounding on the front doors. Jackson had to know something was wrong now. He'd need evidence to prove that Dean Diamant had killed his parents, evidence to prove he was here with her today before he disappeared again.

She needed to get the dean's blood on her.

Reese swallowed hard. Oh, hell, this was not going to be fun.

Yeah, yeah. Bad guy talking. He really wanted her to listen to his whole egotistical speech. That could buy her some time. "I'm going to kill you, Red, because you are more trouble than you're worth."

"Yeah, I've been told I've got a red-haired temperament. I'm a little mouthy. A little independent. A little picky about the man I want to be with."

The moment his foot touched the bottom step, Reese typed in the letters *SOS*, hit Send and ran.

His feet pounded up the stairs behind her as she raced for her office. She shoved her key into the doorknob and cursed. Really? Today was the day the damn lock decided to work? Of course, Dean's keys had made every door as accessible to him as they were to her.

Run!

Leaving her key jammed in the lock, she sprinted backstage. She tipped over the two prop tables behind the set, hoping to create an obstacle course to slow Dean down. But he was gaining on her.

Think!

She couldn't go upstairs. There was only one way in or out of that level. She'd be trapped.

Dean was between her and the back door now.

She wouldn't risk the balcony or catwalk. There were too many places she could trip and fall. Too many ways she could plummet to her death.

She needed a weapon.

"You're just prolonging the inevitable, Red."

She snatched the axe off the prop table on the other side of the stage. It was dull. It was old. Hell, it was fake. But maybe she could at least use it as a club if he got close to her.

She had to make it to the front doors of the auditorium. There was no other way for her to escape.

She charged through the garden doors at the back

of the set and ran straight into Dean. He wrapped his arms tightly around her and pointed the tip of his blade at her neck.

Reese screamed. She never even felt the cut, but she could feel the burning aftereffects of the nick in her skin. She whacked at him with the axe, but it merely knocked his hand away and was jarred from her grip. There was no cut, no blood, except for the ooze trickling down her own neck and dotting the sweater she wore. She needed his blood, not hers!

She locked her chin down to her chest, fighting to keep anything vulnerable from the slice of his blade. She stomped on his feet, gouged at his eyes. But his grip was strong, and he wasn't letting go. She reached behind her head and clawed her fingernails through his cheek.

Victory!

Sort of.

Not.

Enraged by the blood she'd drawn from his face, Dean picked her up and slammed her to the floor. Her head struck the stage, leaving her dazed. He straddled her and grabbed a fistful of her hair, yanking her head back to expose her throat, when it sounded like an explosion had gone off in the lobby.

"What the hell…?" Dean muttered.

It was enough of an interruption to blink her eyes clear and pick up the axe that had dropped at her feet.

Glass shattered and fell like thunderous raindrops. An engine roared in her ears. The entire building shook as she swung that axe with every bit of strength she could muster against the side of his head.

An alarm screeched to life with a deafening pulse-beat, and she heard footsteps charging through the auditorium.

"Reese!"

That voice. That blessed voice.

Jackson Dobbs wasn't just the stronger man here today. He was smarter.

Dean swayed above her for a moment, then turned toward the new threat.

"Get off her, you son of a—"

Reese felt the impact of Jackson tackling Dean and taking him to the floor. While the two men traded kicks and punches and grappled for control of the knife, she rolled over and crawled away to a relatively safe distance. Even though he was armed, Dean was at the disadvantage because Jackson was angry, he was protecting her, and he knew how to fight.

Understanding what *her* job was right now, Reese scrambled to her feet and hurried to her office. Now that she wasn't in a panic, she could turn the key in the lock. She shoved the door open and scanned the room for what she needed. There. Next to the fake stone pediment Zach had built for her. A brown paper sack. She turned it over and dumped the contents before shoving her right hand inside. With her other hand she grabbed the duct tape every good theater company kept in stock. She wound it around the neck of the bag, then sealed it around her wrist.

She snagged a rope that looked like the only real

weapon she could get her hands on and ran back to the stage in time to see Jackson lift Dean by the collar of his shirt and knock the knife away from his limp hand. Then he hauled back his fist and knocked her attacker out cold before he dropped him to the floor.

"I wanted to do that," she complained. "It might not be as satisfying as you knocking him out. But he made me angry. All 'I'm your mentor, you should worship me.' And 'I tried to scare you into loving me.' He said your mother and I aren't the only women he's manipulated like this, either."

"We'll check it out," Jackson wheezed.

"Good. He needs to go away forever."

"Reese—"

"At least let me tie him up in case he comes to again." She knelt beside Dean's prone body and pulled his hands together behind his back. "He's not getting away with killing your parents and trying to kill me."

"What's that?" Jackson sounded slightly winded as he pointed to the bag on her hand.

"Evidence." She held it up while using that elbow and her left hand to tie as many knots as tightly as she could around Dean's wrists. "It's his blood. I preserved it in an evidence bag like you do. You can compare what's under my fingernails to the unidentified blood on that knife. You can prove that Dean killed your parents."

Jackson sat down hard on the top step at the edge of the stage. "Come here," he ordered in a gruff voice. "Come here now."

"This is taking me a minute. With one hand and all. They're just little half-hitches. But I tied a lot of—"

"You said to ask for what I want."

Reese turned to fully look at his proud, battered face. "Huh?"

"I want you here. In my arms. Now."

She supposed seven knots were enough to subdue an unconscious man. Something was off about Jackson's unusually stern demand. She pushed to her feet and knelt beside him, winding her arms around his neck and squeezing as tightly as she dared. "I'm so sorry about before. I didn't want to fight. I never want to scare you away."

"Fat chance of that." His arm snaked around her waist and he lifted her onto his lap. His fingers caressed her neck. "You're bleeding."

"It's just a nick," she assured him. "I did what you said. I fought hard. I fought dirty. Until you could get to me."

"You fought smart. Texting gibberish like that? I knew something was wrong. By the time I got that *SOS*, I'd already found a way to get inside."

When she braced her hand against his stomach to shift to a more comfortable position, he jerked slightly and groaned. Reese scrambled off his lap and inspected the small pool of crimson staining the front of his shirt. "He stabbed you." She nudged his shoulder to get him to lie down flat on the stage and pushed up his shirt to inspect the wound on the left side of his torso. With the evidence bag preventing her from removing her sweater or blouse, Reese kicked off her ankle boot and peeled off a cotton sock, which she then wadded up and pressed against his wound. "Damn it, you big galoot. You aren't supposed to get hurt. Don't die on me."

He reached up to palm the side of her face and neck. "Honey, I'm not dying. I have plans to be here for opening night of your play. And to dance with you at Buck and Chelsea's wedding. And to celebrate with you when you pass your oral exams and get your PhD. I plan to be here to celebrate all the big moments with you. All the little ones, too."

Reese nodded, sniffing back the tears that stung her eyes. "I want that. I want all of that, too. We're going to toast your parents now that you've caught their killer. I want to visit them in the cemetery and tell them what a smart, brave, caring, strong, sexy man their miracle boy has become—how he served his country, how he protects his city, how he saved my life. I want to tell them how much I love him. How much I need him to be there to share all those big and little moments."

"Freckles." He brushed his thumb along the tears streaming down her cheeks. "Don't cry. Give me bad guys and crime scenes any day of the week. But please don't cry."

"Happy tears, Jackson. Happy tears." She pressed a quick, deep kiss to his lips, then went back to concentrating on his wound. "I have no idea where my phone is now. I probably lost it when he tackled me. We need to call for the police and an ambulance."

"Already done."

"You're sure you're not dying? I'll be pissed off if you are."

"I don't think he nicked anything vital. I'm pretty clearheaded."

"You're still going to the hospital."

"Anything you want, it's yours."

"You. I want you."

"You got me. I love you so much, Reese Atkinson. Even when I wasn't sure I knew how to love, I loved you."

"You're damn good at loving me, Jackson. I'm the luckiest woman in Kansas City. In all the world. I love you, too."

"You'll have to use some of that Lowry money to fix the front doors. And maybe my truck."

She looked back to see the wreck of his truck that he'd crashed through the glass doors at the front of the building. There were cops coming in now, KCPD and campus police both.

"One more kiss before we have company."

Reese cupped Jackson's wonderful, scarred, square face and leaned down to very thoroughly kiss him. "All you have to do is ask."

Epilogue

"I love seeing you in a tuxedo," Reese gushed, letting Jackson help her down from the cab of his new truck. Before he straightened her sparkly wool wrap around her shoulders and shut the door, she was reaching up to adjust the knot in his silvery-blue tie. He'd hastily put it on in the truck at the last stoplight on their way to Chelsea and Buck's wedding at the historic Loose Mansion in downtown Kansas City.

"You like seeing me out of it more," he teased, dutifully standing still while she smoothed his tie over his starched shirt and buttoned his navy-blue jacket. Now that her show was over, she and her brilliant, brave, musclebound criminologist had been spending nearly every night together, either at her apartment or his home.

Reese smiled as she straightened the lapels of his jacket. It thrilled her to no end that Jackson was getting comfortable enough with his social skills to actually flirt and share his dry sense of humor with her. "I really do."

Dean Diamant was in jail awaiting trial for the

murder of Jackson's parents as well as stalking and assault charges. The DA's office had taken the death penalty off the table in exchange for information on other victims the dean had stalked and assaulted over the past twenty-three years. But until Dr. Diamant was pronounced guilty and sent to prison for the rest of his life, Jackson had vowed to remain Reese's protector.

While she loved that he wanted to be with her, he'd been a terrible patient, more worried about the fading bruises on her skin instead of allowing her to change the bandages over his own stitches, or wanting to hold her when she had nightmares about her ordeal instead of resting like he should. He'd insisted on attending every performance of the play in the evenings, and working days at the crime lab to pick up the slack from his teammates who were focused on the Diamant case. He'd quizzed her over her dissertation and ridden with her to Grangeport to meet her sister, brother-in-law and nephews instead of staying home to rest. The only time they'd been apart had been those first three nights when the doctors at St. Luke's Medical Center had kept him to pump him full of antibiotics and monitor his recovery from surgery to repair the stab wound that, while it had blessedly missed piercing any vital organs, had torn through skin and muscle and chipped one of his ribs, necessitating that they find and remove the bone fragment before stitching him up.

As if sensing the darker turn of her thoughts and how scared she been at the thought of losing him,

Jackson covered her hands with his, stilling them against his chest to halt the last-minute touch-ups to his formal attire that had become random caresses. "I'm okay."

Pulling herself out of her head, she pressed a kiss to his damaged hand. "I know. Sometimes, I just need to feel for myself that my troubles didn't get you killed."

"Not dead," he assured her. "But if you keep petting me like that, we're going to be even later."

Reese's eyes widened at his guttural warning. Was he saying what she thought he was? "The doctor finally cleared you for *normal* activity at yesterday's appointment. You already conducted a thorough freckle exploration when you came to pick me up this afternoon. That's why we're already running behind to get to the wedding." She felt her brief moment of melancholy dissipate. With a resolute sigh, she smiled to know that this good man was still part of her life. "But I don't think the doctor meant you should have sex multiple times throughout the day now."

"I'm a scientist."

Reese blinked. "What does that have to do with anything?"

The corner of his mouth curled up in that shy smile she loved. "Scientific theory requires multiple tests to prove conclusively what the evidence is saying. While I love sleeping with you cuddled up next to me, I wanted to know if being with you was as good as I remember."

His clinical explanation made her giggle. Her man

was funny. And sweet. And everything she hadn't known she needed. Bracing her hands against his chest, she stretched up on tiptoe, still falling shy of reaching his mouth. When she whimpered in frustration at her inability to touch her lips to his, Jackson lowered his head. Warming at how attentive he was to her wants and needs, she smiled. "And your scientific conclusion?"

"Better every damn time."

Finally, Jackson covered her mouth with his, reminding her of how their lovemaking had started this morning when he'd arrived at her apartment to pick her up for the wedding. And since she was waiting for his help to zip up her dress before putting it on, she had greeted him in little more than her underwear and a robe. Once the door was locked behind him, it hadn't taken much for him to lift her into his arms, back her against the wall and strip her down to her freckles. He'd mussed her hair and the makeup she'd so carefully applied, but Reese didn't care. His callused hands and needy touches made her body sing long before she'd gotten his shirt undone and his slacks and boxer briefs pushed down over his hips. Despite their frantic need to consume each other, he'd entered her slowly, tenderly, lifting her over the crest before he found his release inside her.

"I didn't know it could be like this," he'd whispered against her ear before lowering her feet to the floor. *"I didn't know it was this good when you loved someone. When you can trust them with your heart."*

"Your words are always a treasure to me, Jack-

son Dobbs," she'd said, touching her forehead to his. She tilted her eyes up to his handsome gray eyes. *"But you'd better stop talking before you make me cry and ruin the last of my makeup. I love you, too."* Then she pushed against his chest, knowing he only retreated a step because he'd do almost anything she asked. *"You're an usher, remember? Chelsea will never forgive us if we're late."*

Jackson had nodded. He picked up the robe and satiny panties he'd removed and placed them in her hands before he redressed himself. *"Go. You'll need something warm over your dress. It's cold out."* He'd dropped a kiss to the crown of her hair before shooing her toward her bedroom. *"We're leaving in fifteen minutes."*

"Who needs a coat? I'm plenty warm with you around," she teased. Reese wiggled her bare, freckled butt as she hurried down the hall. Jackson's deep-pitched groan made her feel more beautiful and important to him than any words could.

Now they were hurrying hand-in-hand down the sidewalk as fast as her short legs and tea-length gown allowed. But with Jackson to cling to, she never once stumbled on her strappy high-heels or felt the chilly November wind. Chelsea's eclectic tastes and the World War I era mansion gave the wedding a whole Downton Abbey vibe, and Reese had embraced her new friend's theme by raiding the costume department at the theater for a silvery-blue gown with an antique lace overlay and three-quarter lace sleeves.

"Thank goodness you're here. I was about to text

you." Lexi Callahan-Murphy, Chelsea's matron-of-honor, greeted them at the door. She wore a vintage peach gown and had an uncharacteristic look of panic on her face. "Sorry, Jackson. I need to borrow your date."

He frowned. "Everything okay?"

Lexi flipped her hand back and forth in the universal response for just so-so. "I'm on Plan C right now." She turned her focus down to Reese and pulled her into her arms. "Beautiful dress, by the way."

"Thanks." Reese returned the taller woman's hug, concerned when she felt that Lexi seemed jittery. "You look lovely, too. What can I help with?"

After Lexi sent Jackson off to hang up her wrap and check in with Grayson Malone, the other usher for this evening's ceremony, she grabbed Reese by the hand, and dragged her up the wide mahogany stairs to the bridal suite on the second floor. "Chels doesn't have any family. Allie—Grayson's Allie—is here, too, but she needs to go down and oversee the guest book and gift table because people are already arriving. I'm supposed to be getting Chelsea dressed right now. But I'm not much help."

"Lexi." Reese stopped and squeezed the other woman's hand. Although she was Jackson's supervisor and team leader at the crime lab, she was also their friend. And right now, she looked a little green around the gills. "Stop and take a breath. Are you okay?"

"It's nothing contagious." Lexi clutched her hand

against her stomach and inhaled a deep breath with Reese. Then another.

Not what she'd asked, but okay. "Better?"

Lexi nodded before pushing open the door to the bridal suite.

"Oh good, you're back. Hey, Reese. Glad you could make it." The bride-to-be stood in front of a full-length mirror while Allie Tate, Grayson's girlfriend, fastened the many buttons down the back of Chelsea O'Brien's ivory lace gown. Reese blinked against the sparkle of jewelry on Allie's hand as Chelsea pushed her silver glitter-framed glasses up onto the bridge of her nose and glanced at the clock on the wall. 5:30 p.m. "Buck is a stickler for punctuality. And it may take the next thirty minutes just to get me dressed."

Reese quickly took in the clock, the worried bride, the two miniature poodles lounging on the sofa who were dressed in blue satin vests that matched the wedding party's ties, the short veil draped over a hanger in front of the window and the way Lexi hunched over and pressed the back of her hand to her lips. These women—Jackson's friends and now hers—needed help. Reese rubbed her hands together. "I've been making quick changes in dressing rooms for years. What do you need?"

Chelsea counted off the tasks on her fingers. "Rings tied to dog's vests. Boutonnieres pinned on Buck, his son and the ushers. Allie needs to run downstairs to greet the guests. Veil on my head. Figure out what's wrong with Lexi and get me downstairs to marry Buck."

Lexi picked up the ring boxes on the dresser. "I've got the dogs."

Allie, an athletic, statuesque blonde, handed off button duty to Reese. "If you take over here, I'll bring the boutonnieres to the guys and get them pinned up on my way downstairs to the guest table."

"Of course." Reese had three more buttons fastened before she heard the moaning noise behind her.

She and Chelsea turned to see Lexi grabbing her purse and dashing out the door. "I... Oh... Sorry."

Chelsea squeezed Reese's hand and urged her to follow her matron of honor. "I can at least get the dogs ready. Go. Make sure she's okay."

With a nod, Reese hurried after Lexi and followed her down the hallway. En route, she pulled her phone from the pocket of her dress and texted Jackson.

Is Aiden around? Lexi isn't feeling well. We're in the women's upstairs bathroom.

She pushed open the bathroom door to the sound of Lexi dry heaving in one of the stalls. Reese wet several towels with cool water and handed them to Lexi when she came out. Wow, she looked pale. "Here."

"Thank you." Lexi dabbed at her lips, then pressed the cool towels to the back of her neck before pointing to her bag on the counter beside the sink. "Would you mind? There are some crackers in there."

Reese couldn't help grinning as she opened the bag of crackers and handed one to the other woman. "This isn't the flu or something you ate, is it. My sister went through this with both of her babies. Are congratulations in order?"

Lexi nibbled on the cracker and nodded. "We haven't announced it yet. I wanted to wait until I was three months along. But this morning sickness is no joke."

"Um, it's not morning." Reese led her over to a wooden stool at the end of the row of sinks.

"Exactly. I don't think my body understands the concept of morning sickness. It thinks it's okay to do this all day long."

Lexi's color looked better as she polished off the cracker and rested a moment. "Anything else I can do to help?"

"Just make sure Chels is downstairs at six. She's waited months to marry Buck. I don't think she'll survive if she has to put it off any longer. I'll make sure I'm down there with my bouquet. I just need a few minutes to rest and get my equilibrium back."

"You got it."

There was a sharp knock at the door before it opened slightly and Blue, her husband's K-9 partner, trotted in and went straight to Lexi and laid his head in her lap. Said husband, Aiden, poked his head in. "Lex? You all right? Can I come in?"

Reese smiled at Lexi, petted the dog and opened the door wider. "It's all clear. Go on in." She squeezed Aiden's arm on her way out. "Congratulations." He winked his thanks and went in to take care of his pregnant wife.

Just like preparing for the opening curtain of a show, the last minutes before the ceremony flew by.

Reese breathed a sigh of relief as she slipped into the row of chairs near the back of the high-ceilinged garden room beside Jackson right as the music changed to start the wedding. Chelsea was dressed, beautiful, and ready for the crime lab's boss, Mac Taylor, to walk her down the aisle. Buck's grown son, Clark, had leashes for the dogs, and walked them up to the wide mahogany fireplace at the front of the room before removing the rings and standing beside his father as best man. Then, Aiden and Blue walked Lexi into the room. She looked every bit the radiant mother-to-be now after some rest, a snack and some TLC from her husband. Finally, everyone stood as the wedding march played and Chelsea and Mac entered.

Being vertically challenged, once the bride and her stand-in father had walked past, Reese had no view of what was happening at the front of the room. When laughter and a smattering of applause rippled through the rows of guests, Reese tugged on Jackson's arm. "What's going on? I can't see."

"Buck kissed her."

At the minister's request, they all sat down. "He's supposed to wait until the end of the ceremony."

Grayson spoke from his chair on the opposite side of Allie, who sat next to Reese. "I wouldn't tell a man what he can and can't do on his wedding day."

When he squeezed Allie's hand and pressed a kiss to her temple, the glint of something shiny that she'd seen upstairs registered. Reese pressed her hands together in silent applause and whispered, "That's an engagement ring. Congratulations, you two."

"My Thanksgiving present," Allie explained. "We don't want to steal the spotlight from Chelsea and Buck, so we haven't announced it yet." Reese pantomimed locking her mouth shut and throwing away the key, ensuring she'd keep their secret. Allie looked back at Grayson, who studied her just as intently. "But when my Marine asked, I didn't hesitate to say yes."

"Love you, Lieutenant," Grayson whispered.

"Love you." The couple exchanged a soft kiss.

Jackson stretched his hand in front of Reese to shake Grayson's hand in a silent congratulations. When he saw how Reese was craning her neck to see the ceremony at the front of the room, her big guy simply picked her up out of her chair and sat her on his lap. She settled her hands atop his forearms where they wound around her waist and watched the rest of the wedding surrounded by his warmth and love.

A pregnancy, an engagement and a wedding. Reese was happy for her friends, and even happier that Jackson felt included as an important part of his friends' lives.

But she couldn't help but wonder if he believed he deserved all those things for himself, too. And if he truly understood how much she wanted to be the woman who shared those life-changing events with him.

JACKSON COULDN'T BE happier for his friends. And while he was honored to be a part of their lives, he wondered if he would ever find that kind of lifelong happiness for himself. He loved Reese, and he believed she loved him. But he was too used to being alone, too used to being the outcast for him to completely believe that she was his for the long haul— that she'd want his babies, that she'd marry him.

Even now, at the reception where Buck and Chelsea and Grayson and Allie had danced nearly every dance together, while Aiden had sat Lexi in a quiet corner to take care of her needs, he sat at a table with Chelsea's pseudo-grandpa, Vinnie Goring, while Reese continued to help Chelsea with her dress and other needs. She chatted with many of the guests, whether she knew them or not, smiled at everyone. Reese was comfortable with crowds and parties, comfortable with people, while he sat off to the side like a growly, oversize version of a wallflower.

He was proud of Reese for stepping up to help his friends this evening. She'd sat by his side through the ceremony and dinner afterward, so everyone here knew she was with him. But he wanted to be in her circle of light, to be part of her world and have her goodness shine in his heart…forever.

But how did he make that happen? Where did he find the words he'd never needed before?

Vinnie Goring wasn't at a loss for words, though. The older gentleman leaned his cane against the table, sipped a drink from his bottle of beer, and continued on, as if Jackson had been focused on him and not the thoughts and frustrations and dreams going back and forth inside his head. "If I could have done, I'd have walked my Ladybug down the aisle. But now that

I've got to have the other knee worked on, I'm lucky I'm here at all. Doesn't look like I'll be able to keep the bar going, either. That first father-daughter dance about did me in." Vinnie muttered a curse. "Made me cry in front of everybody. Chels is a good girl. She's gonna let me move into her house since it's all one level, when she moves in with Buck. His son, Clark, is going to help me take care of all the animals while Buck and Chelsea are on their honeymoon." Vinnie exhaled a deep breath. "And I'm boring you to tears, aren't I, young man?" He set his drink down with enough force that Jackson turned and gave the man a quizzical look. Vinnie grinned and nodded his head to the left. "You're a good listener. Though I expect you've got other things on your mind tonight."

Jackson turned to follow the older man's unspoken message. Reese was making her way across the room to him, boldly, with a smile Jackson felt all the way down to his soul. Just like that first day she'd come to the crime lab to give him the bloodied knife that had led to solving his parents' murders, she approached him. *Him. He* was the man she wanted to see.

He was vaguely aware of Vinnie exchanging pleasantries with Reese. He stood when she held out her hand to him. She tilted her head, her gaze never leaving his. "Dance with me?"

Jackson had never danced with a woman before. Even in middle school P.E. where he'd learned the basics, he'd been on his own. At the wide-eyed hesitation that must have been on his face, Reese tugged on his hand. "Hold me in your arms on the dance floor and sway back and forth. You can handle that right?"

When he grunted, she rolled her eyes and laughed. And then her hips were locked against his thighs, and she was in his arms. She tipped her head back and rested her chin against his chest, looking up at him with a smile that made him feel gooey and vulnerable and strong as an ox. "Yeah. This is what I needed."

He lowered his head to steal a kiss and then she tucked her head beneath his chin. He pulled the hand he held into his chest and matched his rhythm to the gentle, mesmerizing sway of her hips. They danced together through two slow tunes, a soft country ballad and an instrumental classic. When the third song started and Reese sang softly against him, Jackson knew he didn't want his time with her to ever end. He'd always wanted what his parents had had together, and Reese Atkinson was the first woman—the only woman—he'd ever believed could be his. The only woman who made him believe he could be hers.

Abruptly, he stopped. He released her to frame her face between his hands. "Do you want to get a dog with me?"

Reese stopped, blinking in confusion. "A dog? Is this like the pie thing?"

If he had a third hand, he would have whacked himself in the back of the head. Not exactly what he'd meant to say. Her gaze narrowed as more words spewed out of his mouth. "There's this place just outside the city called Shadow Protectors Ranch.

They rescue and train dogs. I'd like you to have one to be with you during those late nights at the theater when I can't be with you. We'd practically be living together since we'd be sharing ownership of the dog, and the responsibility of caring for..."

Reese pressed her fingers against his lips to silence him. "Are you asking me to move in with you?" He'd meant to say something like that. Her beautiful violet blue eyes studied him for a long moment. "Is that what you really want to ask?"

He was breathing too hard. This moment had suddenly gotten too big for him to contain. "Elope to Vegas with me."

Her eyes widened and color flooded the freckles on her cheeks.

No. He'd done this all wrong. She'd want a big event like Chelsea's wedding. She'd want her sister and family there. All their friends. She'd be so beautiful in a fancy formal gown.

"Yes."

"Yes?" The doubts that had held his heart in check for too many years disappeared in the light of Reese's smile.

"I'll marry you. In Vegas or wherever. If you could wait until the semester is over. I'm thinking maybe Christmas break. Then we'd have time for a honeymoon afterward."

Jackson stopped her planning by lowering his head and kissing her. He crushed her in his arms, lifted her feet off the floor and kissed her again. Reese responded with a matching passion. Her kindness and understanding and need made him feel like the luckiest man in the room. They stood and kissed in the middle of the dance floor until one of his friends good-naturedly shouted at them to get a room.

Jackson reluctantly broke off the kiss and lowered Reese back to the floor. He felt like shouting above the noise and music of the room. He wanted to tell someone, everyone, that Reese Atkinson was his. That he'd asked in his own way, and she'd said yes.

Then she tugged on his lapels and demanded that he look her in the eye. "Until then, I'm moving in, we're sleeping together, and we are totally getting that dog. Are you okay with all that?"

Jackson grunted his happiness and kissed her again.

* * * * *

Look for the previous books in
USA TODAY *bestselling author*
Julie Miller's Kansas City Crime Lab series:

K-9 Patrol
Decoding the Truth
The Evidence Next Door

Available now wherever
Harlequin Intrigue books are sold!

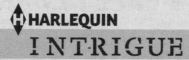
#2193 COLD CASE IDENTITY
Hudson Sibling Solutions • by Nicole Helm

Palmer Hudson has a history of investigating cold case crimes. Helping his little sister's best friend, Louisa O'Brien, uncover the truth about her biological parents should be simple. But soon their investigation becomes a dangerous mystery...complicated by an attraction neither can deny.

#2194 MONSTER IN THE MARSH
The Swamp Slayings • by Carla Cassidy

When businessman Jackson Fortier meets Josie Cadieux, a woman who now lives deep in the swamp, he agrees to help find the mysterious man who assaulted her a year earlier. Soon, Josie's entry into polite upper-crust society to expose the culprit changes Jackson's role from investigator to protector.

#2195 K-9 SECURITY
New Mexico Guard Dogs • by Nichole Severn

Rescuing lone survivor Elena Navarro from a deadly cartel attack sends Cash Meyers's bodyguard instincts into overdrive. The former marine—and his trusty K-9 partner—will be damned if she falls prey a second time...even if he loses his heart keeping her safe.

#2196 HELICOPTER RESCUE
Big Sky Search and Rescue • by Danica Winters

After a series of strange disappearances, jaded helicopter pilot Casper Keller joins forces with Kristin Lauren, a mysterious woman involved in his father's death. But fighting the elements, sabotage and a mission gone astray may pale in comparison to the feelings their reluctant partnership exposes...

#2197 A STALKER'S PREY
West Investigations • by K.D. Richards

Actress Bria Baker is being stalked. And her ex, professional bodyguard Xavier Nichols, is her best hope for finishing her movie safely. With Bria's star burning as hot as her chemistry with Xavier, her stalker is convinced it's time for Bria to be his...

#2198 THE SHERIFF'S TO PROTECT
by Janice Kay Johnson

Savannah Baird has been raising her niece since her troubled brother's disappearance. But when his dead body is discovered—and unknown entities start making threats—hiding out at officer Logan Quade's isolated ranch is their only chance at survival...and her brother's only chance at justice.

Get 3 FREE REWARDS!

We'll send you 2 FREE Books plus a FREE Mystery Gift.

FREE Value Over **$20**

Both the **Harlequin Intrigue®** and **Harlequin® Romantic Suspense** series feature compelling novels filled with heart-racing action-packed romance that will keep you on the edge of your seat.

YES! Please send me 2 FREE novels from the Harlequin Intrigue or Harlequin Romantic Suspense series and my FREE gift (gift is worth about $10 retail). After receiving them, if I don't wish to receive any more books, I can return the shipping statement marked "cancel." If I don't cancel, I will receive 6 brand-new Harlequin Intrigue Larger-Print books every month and be billed just $6.49 each in the U.S. or $6.99 each in Canada, a savings of at least 13% off the cover price, or 4 brand-new Harlequin Romantic Suspense books every month and be billed just $5.49 each in the U.S. or $6.24 each in Canada, a savings of at least 12% off the cover price. It's quite a bargain! Shipping and handling is just 50¢ per book in the U.S. and $1.25 per book in Canada.* I understand that accepting the 2 free books and gift places me under no obligation to buy anything. I can always return a shipment and cancel at any time by calling the number below. The free books and gift are mine to keep no matter what I decide.

Choose one:
☐ **Harlequin Intrigue Larger-Print** (199/399 BPA GRMX)
☐ **Harlequin Romantic Suspense** (240/340 BPA GRMX)
☐ **Or Try Both!** (199/399 & 240/340 BPA GRQD)

Name (please print)

Address | Apt. #

City | State/Province | Zip/Postal Code

Email: Please check this box ☐ if you would like to receive newsletters and promotional emails from Harlequin Enterprises ULC and its affiliates. You can unsubscribe anytime.

Mail to the **Harlequin Reader Service:**
IN U.S.A.: P.O. Box 1341, Buffalo, NY 14240-8531
IN CANADA: P.O. Box 603, Fort Erie, Ontario L2A 5X3

Want to try 2 free books from another series! Call 1-800-873-8635 or visit www.ReaderService.com.

*Terms and prices subject to change without notice. Prices do not include sales taxes, which will be charged (if applicable) based on your state or country of residence. Canadian residents will be charged applicable taxes. Offer not valid in Quebec. This offer is limited to one order per household. Books received may not be as shown. Not valid for current subscribers to the Harlequin Intrigue or Harlequin Romantic Suspense series. All orders subject to approval. Credit or debit balances in a customer's account(s) may be offset by any other outstanding balance owed by or to the customer. Please allow 4 to 6 weeks for delivery. Offer available while quantities last.

Your Privacy—Your information is being collected by Harlequin Enterprises ULC, operating as Harlequin Reader Service. For a complete summary of the information we collect, how we use this information and to whom it is disclosed, please visit our privacy notice located at corporate.harlequin.com/privacy-notice. From time to time we may also exchange your personal information with reputable third parties. If you wish to opt out of this sharing of your personal information, please visit readerservice.com/consumerchoice or call 1-800-873-8635. **Notice to California Residents**—Under California law, you have specific rights to control and access your data. For more information on these rights and how to exercise them, visit corporate.harlequin.com/california-privacy.

HIHRS23